DEADLY
SANCTION

DEADLY
SANCTION

ROGER ELWOOD

WORD PUBLISHING
Dallas • London • Vancouver • Melbourne

Library of Congress Cataloging-in-Publication Data

Elwood, Roger.
　　Deadly sanction / Roger Elwood.
　　　　p.　cm.—(The OSS chronicles)
　　ISBN 0–8499–3387–0
　　1. World War, 1939–1945—Fiction.　I. Title.
　II. Series: Elwood, Roger.　OSS Chronicles.
　PS3555.L85D4　1993
　813'.54—dc20　　　　　　　　　　　　　　　　　　93–11024
　　　　　　　　　　　　　　　　　　　　　　　　　　CIP

34569　LBM　987654321

Printed in the United States of America

To Sharon Paul—

With every wish
that the years ahead
bring the best
life has to offer

Preface

I owe the existence of this series, of which *Deadly Sanction* is the second entry, entirely to the dedicated efforts of two individuals at Word: Joey Paul and Lee Gessner. Both men championed it to such an extent that our mutual enthusiasm caught on with others in crucial departments at Word. I owe these two men a great deal because I am finding these books, in which we all are putting a great deal of time and hard work, to be among the most intriguing I have been able to write, for the World War II period holds unparalleled fascination, as far as I am concerned, with many colorful heroes and a whole roster of the worst villains in the history of the human race.

It is sobering to realize that, while we can rejoice over the Churchills, the Eisenhowers, and others, the bad guys also did exist, and their most demonic deeds could never be overstated, no matter how dramatic a novel concerning them tries to be. The key in any historical series is not to glorify them through the very process of showing how evil the Hitlers, Himmlers, Heydrichs, and others were.

There were *obvious* heroes and obvious villains but one of the more memorable discoveries a writer can make during the course of research is the existence of those about whom conventional wisdom is faulty at best. The Nazi hierarchy, for example, was chockfull of heroes whom the media of today should spotlight far more than has been the case. These were men—generals, admirals, and others—who were as repulsed by the atrocities of the Nazi regime as were those fighting with the Allies.

The main thrust of *Deadly Sanction* has to do with just such an individual, someone who could have been one of history's most heroic figures if he had acted more decisively. Nevertheless, he remains someone who deserves far more attention than the barbaric leaders he came to loathe.

Roger Elwood

Prologue

Lina Heydrich sat on the veranda of a borrowed home, enjoying for a few moments the clear air, the warm overhead summer sun beating down on a face that had become more wrinkled in a matter of a year or so than in all the time that preceded this period, a face now crowned by hair, once pure blonde, that had become streaked with gray strands and suddenly was as lifeless to the touch as Lina herself.

The property provided for her by the National Socialists was spacious, adorned by attractive shrubbery on the grounds, as well as fine antique furniture in the gable-style house itself, and furthermore, she was waited on by a staff of vigilant servants from the moment she arose each morning until she retired to bed at night. Yet she could never allow herself to fall into the trap of considering this new residence as permanent. It was simply part of a transitional time in her life, a time of getting used to being without the only man who had ever mattered to her.

"Reinhard . . . ," she whispered, her voice heavy with melancholy. "The sweetest man God ever created."

The children had been sent off to a special Nazi Youth summer camp. Not having them by her side emphasized her sense of pervading loneliness.

Her gaze drifted to a round wooden table in front of her. Piled on top were photographs that she had specifically requested from Heinrich Himmler. She picked up a handful and leafed through them one at a time.

"There is still justice in this world," Lina mumbled. "There is yet some measure of vengeance."

She saw men and women being shot to death.

"Jew lovers!" she spat out those two words as though she had just tasted something oppressively bitter.

Other photographs showed scores of bodies in ditches with lime being poured over them, covering their frozen expressions of pain.

"At least you will fertilize some beautiful plants!" she exclaimed triumphantly.

She had asked Himmler to let her pick out the flowers and he had agreed. She wanted ones with the brightest colors and the sweetest scents.

Now, months later, she had just returned from Lidice, after walking barefoot among the blossoms and inhaling the fragrant air into her lungs.

"People *will* remember, dearest Reinhard," she had said then, her head tilted back, the sun's rays warming her cheeks. "There are stone memorials all over this country that pay homage to your memory, but I wanted something in addition, something alive and colorful to celebrate what you meant to so many . . . especially me."

She became bored by the photographs and was about to put them neatly back in a file folder when she noticed that one had fallen on the grass at her feet.

The focus wasn't sharp, but the image was clear enough to infuriate her. From the photograph a tall, sandy-haired man looked back at her with large, deep-set hazel eyes that seemed both warm and unfailingly confident. His strong, angular features made him seem younger than she knew he was, and although she loathed him for what he had done, she could not help a passing hint of physical desire as she once again scanned this out-of-focus image of his firm, athletically trained body.

"Bartlett!" she said, her voice nearly a shout.

Lina was tempted to take it between her fingers and tear it into the tiniest of pieces, but she stopped herself from giving in to this impulse, deciding instead that it would be better to be able to look at the photo and remind herself of every inch of that face.

"I want to personally rip the flesh off it," she growled. "I want to use your skull as a paperweight. I want to—"

Her entire body was shaking.

Moments later, she had brought herself under control, her German discipline kicking in; she started to return that last photo to the folder. Neatly hand-printed on the back was a modicum of facts that seemed every bit as familiar to her as those from her own life. She recited them from memory: *Stephen Bartlett* . . . *His wife's name is Natalie* . . . *They have a young son named Andrew.*

Her pulse quickening in anticipation, Lina Heydrich closed her eyes for a moment as she thought that, with any good fortune at all, she could be responsible for shedding *their* blood as well. She was convinced that only then would the man for whom her love would never die . . . only then would the Butcher of Prague be adequately avenged, and she could walk those Lidicean fields of fresh flowers with a heart finally at peace.

1

Even Winston Churchill acknowledged that his beloved England was in a precarious position.

"We cannot *possibly* guarantee the integrity of every inch of British shoreline!" he bellowed as he held the communiqué that had been sent from a source high within the Nazi command center in Berlin. "We do not have nearly enough ships, particularly since we were forced to eliminate the Vichy French fleet so it would not fall into German hands. We do not have enough planes. And we cannot deploy an adequate number of troops for any such task. They can hit us from the air and from the sea. While we will continue to do the best a nation of valor can possibly accomplish, nevertheless . . ."

Churchill was in his office at No. 10 Downing Street with an aide awaiting any command he might spew forth.

"Get in touch with Stephen Bartlett immediately," he said at a near-shout. "Warn him. Get him and his family out of that house before it's too late. We cannot lose such a man! *We cannot!*"

"I anticipated what you were going to say," admitted the aide, a short young man with a complexion nearly ruined by the ravages of acne.

"And you called without waiting for me to say it?" Churchill replied without emotion, trying to appear stern but actually quite pleased at the gumption of someone of such youth.

"The telephone line is dead, sir. I suspect it's been cut."

Churchill's normally red-tinged cheeks lost their color.

"Get some troops out there now!" he ordered. "Send whatever it takes to do what is necessary. Or did you also—?"

The aide nodded.

Churchill had the ability to examine a man from head to foot in a matter of seconds and form an opinion of him that was eerily on the mark.

"Is it possible that every member of your family is like you, young man?" he asked approvingly.

"It does seem so, sir. Rather a pushy lot, we are."

"Do not ever change," Churchill said as he turned away, uncomfortable with giving even that much praise to a callow subordinate.

The aide thanked him and hurried from the office.

Prime Minister Winston Churchill picked up a file from his desk. It was labeled: STEPHEN BARTLETT . . . AMERICAN O.S.S. AGENT.

"I pray . . . ," he started to say out loud, his normally strong voice trembling a bit, "I pray that we are not too late."

In their temporary home in the English countryside, Natalie Bartlett heard the nearby sounds as she was tucking her son Andrew into bed that night.

"Mom?" he said, his freckled face showing sudden fear. "Did you—?"

"Yes," she said, brushing back the sleek black hair that slipped over her cheek as she leaned to kiss her young son. She put a finger to her lips.

"Dad . . . where's Dad?" eight-year-old Andrew whispered.

"I thought he was taking his usual walk," she answered. Natalie sat down beside him on the bed, curling her long, thin legs beneath her. Listening, their eyes locked—hers so round and dark, his lighter and deep set, so like his father's.

They had heard the sounds of somebody stepping in mud and nearly stumbling, followed by a brief spurt of careless, impromptu cursing. These sounds reached their ears from the open window in Andrew's room. Earlier in the day, the English countryside had been buffeted by one of the usual winter rain storms. Bare dirt was quickly changed into quicksand-like mud. Nighttime darkness hid the more treacherous sections around the house.

"So near, Mom," Andrew added, his eyes wide. "So—"

Suddenly the white-painted window frame shattered as machine-gun fire was sprayed against it.

Natalie felt sudden pain in her left shoulder and fell to the floor in a flurry of broken glass, wood splinters, and chunks of plaster.

An instant later, loud voices sounded outside.

Andrew glimpsed a pair of hands reaching through the jagged remains of where the window had been.

"If they're not dead, kill them!" someone shouted.

Andrew saw nothing to defend himself with except one particularly long, thin piece of glass. He grabbed part of the blanket from his bed, wrapping it around one end of the jagged slither. As a very large man started to climb through the window into the bedroom, the eight-year-old lunged forward and jabbed it into whatever part of the intruder's bulk he could reach, which happened to be his neck.

The man fell back, half inside the house, half outside.

He turned and looked at Andrew, an expression of pain mixed with pure hatred smeared across his face along with flecks of blood and dirt. He struggled to stand but only flailed helplessly. Then he gasped once, his body going limp.

Other noises!

The front door being battered, then torn off its hinges.

Andrew glanced at his mother, who was moaning now. Then he heard footsteps down the hallway leading to his bedroom.

He jumped to his feet, slammed the door shut, locked it.

An ax smashed through the center of it, tearing open a hole large enough for a man's big hand.

Andrew hesitated. There were no more suitable glass shards.

His hunting knife!

It was in a chest where he had thrown some toys, games, a couple of wartime souvenirs. He lunged for it, throwing open the lid, rummaging inside, finding the knife with its serrated edge just as the bedroom door was split in half and another large body barreled through and toward him.

And stopped in the center of the floor.

Outside, the sounds of a struggle . . .

Just over the body that was still suspended in the remains of the window, Andrew saw two men fighting; he recognized one of them as his father.

Wearing a stocking mask, the man in front of him took that moment of distraction to reach out and grab Andrew and toss him to one side.

"You killed Klaus!" he screamed. "You shall die as well. But not before I tear out the woman's heart."

He turned in the direction of the female body on the floor.

Andrew dove at his right leg, jabbing the knife into the back of it again and again. Crying out from the pain, the man collapsed, hitting the back of his head on a small square table next to the bed.

Outside, there were no more sounds . . . only the silence of that lonely stretch of land remained.

Andrew crawled to his mother's side. Her eyes were open now.

"Mom, I'm going outside," he told her. "I've got to see what's happened. I think Dad came back and was fighting one of the guys but . . . but I don't hear anything now."

She nodded weakly, unable to speak, but a slight smile crossed her face.

He kissed her on the forehead, and got to his feet. As he was about to climb over the body of the second intruder, he noticed a pistol in a holster strapped to his side.

Dad's taught me to shoot just about everything, he thought. *Mom's been objecting right along, but I'm glad he did!*

He grabbed the gun, hesitating as he felt the weight of it and wondering if an eight-year-old such as himself could hold it still long enough to aim the weapon properly and get off a few rounds.

Don't have much choice, he decided.

He walked cautiously down the hallway to the front entrance; the door hung loosely on one of its hinges.

Once outside, he realized that he was still in his pajamas, hardly enough clothes for the chill evening winds.

Someone shouting!

Andrew could see nothing as his eyes searched the countryside. He ran to the rear of the house and looked again in front of him as far as he could see.

A hundred yards away, that particular stretch of land ended at the edge of a cliff. Against that cliff Andrew could just make out his father's familiar form. Six feet tall, with the muscular frame of an athlete, Stephen Bartlett was in a fight that apparently had gone from near the house to that much farther away.

"*Dad!*" he yelled.

Both men turned for an instant in his direction.

"Go back, son!" Bartlett yelled.

The two were very large men, but the intruder actually was taller and broader. Returning his attention immediately to Bartlett, he managed to lift Bartlett's more than two hundred pounds off the ground by his neck.

Andrew quickly raised the pistol, aimed it at the other man, pulled the trigger, and missed. Startled, the intruder contemptuously threw Bartlett to one side and advanced toward the eight-year-old.

Andrew aimed the heavy pistol again and fired, this time accurately, the bullet hitting the man in the chest. He was flung backward, toward the cliff. For an instant his body seemed to be frozen, moving in no direction at all, and then he tumbled over the edge.

Stephen Bartlett saw his short, pajama-clad son drop the pistol and run toward him, his sandy hair flying in the night wind. The two of them embraced. Bartlett dropped his head to peer into his son's warm, hazel eyes, so much like his own.

"Mom's bad," Andrew cried. "I don't know if she's going to make it. I think she's lost a lot of blood."

"Where were the guards?" his father asked. "I passed them on my way out for my walk. What happened to them? Where could the attackers have been hiding?"

Not expecting Andrew to know the answer, he turned and ran back to the house, pulling Andrew along with him. As they started in through the back door, Stephen Bartlett noticed a body that had been placed among some bushes to his left.

Where could the attackers have been hiding? that thought raced through his mind without letup. *Where—?*

Inside, he saw that his son's assessment of his mother's condition was correct. Natalie Bartlett had to have expert medical help as soon as possible. He knew he could stop the bleeding temporarily but there had to be significant internal damage, and correcting that required the skill of doctors at a major institution such as Charing Cross Hospital.

As he tended to the wound with ice and gauze and some light antiseptic, which was all he could find, he thought back to the assassination of Reinhard Heydrich, the Butcher of Prague, realizing that this attack upon his family and himself had to have come directly as a result of what the Allies celebrated as a triumph but which the Nazis termed a tragedy for Aryans everywhere.

Hitler and Himmler must be having a—, he started to tell himself.

A chill suddenly gripped him.

He glanced at Andrew.

"Dad, what is it?" the boy asked.

"Nothing, son . . . just thinking how important it is that the three of us stay together."

But it was more than that. Bartlett was also recalling stark images of Lina Heydrich and her son. Something cold and dark inside him changed his mind about Hitler and Himmler. Those two maniacs wouldn't necessarily go so far as sending assassins to wipe out the entire Bartlett family, although their restraint would be out of political reality, not any lingering bits and pieces of human decency. But the sorrowing widow of Reinhard Heydrich may have been capable of whatever her vengeful passion could concoct.

Bartlett picked up his wounded and bleeding wife as gently as he could and carried her outside to the old Rover that the British government had loaned him as his personal vehicle while he remained in the country.

Oh, Lord, he prayed, *if only they have done nothing to the motor!*

He opened the back door and stretched Natalie out over the narrow seat. Then he rushed to the front of the car and lifted the hood.

Untouched.

"Maybe they walked in, Dad," Andrew suggested. "Maybe they thought of using this as their getaway car."

Bartlett appreciated his son's precocious intelligence.

"If they walked, where from?" he asked out loud.

"That farmhouse two miles away," Andrew offered.

"But the guards would have seen them coming."

Bartlett shook his head, dismissing any more speculation until long after they had gotten Natalie to safe quarters at Charing Cross.

The Rover started on the second try, belching foul-smelling exhaust.

As he was about to pull away onto the narrow road, he realized he had no weapons with him.

"Andrew," Bartlett said, "I need to get some guns. Stay here, please."

His son sat without protest.

Bartlett smiled, then got out of the car and approached the house cautiously, not knowing if he would find any surprises inside.

He did, but not at all what he expected; he came upon the dead body of the disguised intruder in Andrew's bedroom.

"Let's see who you are," he whispered as he grabbed the mask and pulled it off.

One of the guards assigned by Churchill's own chief of security!

"You killed your partner," Bartlett reasoned, "and then it was clear sailing for the other guys."

That left the question of how Nazi agents could have infiltrated British security to such an extent!

He walked back into the hallway and into his own bedroom, which had a hidden compartment in the wall behind a tall chest of drawers.

Inside were rifles, pistols, grenades.

He grabbed one of each, picking out handguns with the greatest stopping power. Hesitating for a moment, he thought better of his selections and added two more grenades.

Then Bartlett slid the panel across the compartment and moved the chest in front of it again.

After hurrying outside, he reached the Rover and handed the rifle and pistol to his son while placing the grenades between the two of them on the front seat.

He glanced for a moment back at his wife. She remained unconscious. He could see what had been, minutes earlier, just a relatively thin red spot on the white gauze he had managed to wrap tightly over her wound.

"Thank God . . . ," he whispered.

The bleeding had stopped.

"Gunfire," Winston Churchill was being told by the nervous voice at the other end of the phone line. "One of our patrol boats was in the water just beyond where Bartlett and his family have been staying. It came from a heavy-caliber gun. Everything else was quiet. It could be heard clearly, Sir."

Churchill's ample frame was trembling with anger.

"How could this have happened?" he demanded. "We had guards. There was tight security. Launch an investigation immediately."

"Agreed, sir," the voice replied. "I am afraid that the Nazis have a mole somewhere inside No. 10 Downing Street."

Cold sweat suddenly covered Churchill's wide forehead.

"Right now, I want you to send out whatever men and equipment you need to find and protect that family. Contact the captain of that patrol boat. See if he is in a position to help. *Something* must be done! We owe Stephen Bartlett a great deal."

"As you have ordered, sir," the voice said. "But it might be too late, you know."

Churchill slammed the receiver back on its cradle.

. . . it might be too late, you know.

He stood with some effort, his weight and the arthritis that had taken hold making every movement increasingly painful, even with the use of his ever-present cane.

Oh, those newsreel shots of me walking about with such ease, he thought. *No one knows how I suffered after the cameras were shut down. Roosevelt and I both have pain that the public cannot be allowed to learn of just now.*

He thought of the American president.

But he is so much worse, poor man. I cannot say that he will live out this war . . .

Churchill had a photograph of the Bartlett family on a shelf in the bookcase at the opposite end of his wood-paneled office. Now he approached it with something not unlike reverence.

"You have done the impossible, my friend," he said out loud. "You have found a topic about which de Gaulle and I can agree."

And that topic was Stephen Bartlett himself.

"Nothing can be allowed to harm you," Churchill added. "You are too precious to too many of us for any . . ."

He could go not on.

If de Gaulle can cry at the very same thought, I shall not be ashamed of my own tears, he told himself as he took a handkerchief and washed his cheeks before anyone could enter his office and see him like that.

The phone on his desk rang.

Churchill turned and walked as fast as he could over to it. Clearing his throat, he picked up the receiver.

"Yes, what is it?" he growled in trademark fashion.

"There is a report of an automobile exploding into flames only a few miles from where the Bartletts have been staying," the same voice told him. "We are investigating, sir. We do suspect that it was the Rover we gave them."

"Is there anything else?" Churchill asked, sensing the other's hesitation.

"We may have lost them, sir. We may have lost all three!"

Churchill ended the conversation abruptly and dropped the receiver, letting it dangle from its cord.

Getting down on his knees was an ordeal, the pain intense, but he did it just the same, crying out once as they made contact with the floor.

He brought his hands together and wrapped them around one another.

"Oh, Holy Father, I have but one petition this day . . . ," he began.

After he had finished, he opened his eyes and his gaze settled momentarily on that photograph at the other end of the room.

"Any power I wield can go only so far, my dear Stephen," muttered Winston Churchill. "After that, quite Another must take over."

2

Stephen Bartlett saw the grenade, apparently thrown from the heavily wooded area on either side of the road, the familiar small gray object hitting the front of the Rover's hood and bouncing off.

Three seconds before it exploded!

He quickly swerved to the right, the vehicle hitting a ditch, bouncing along it, and then lurching into a thick-trunked tree. The front was badly smashed, its engine pushed partway into the passengers' compartment. Directly behind him, there was an explosion that shuddered through the wounded metal frame of the Rover.

Then the unmistakable odor of gasoline . . . .

"Out of here!" Bartlett yelled.

"I'll help you with Mom," Andrew replied.

"Head into the woods, son. I'll take care of your mother."

The boy obeyed, throwing open the door on his side and dashing out.

Bartlett tried to do the same with the one next to him.

Jammed!

He tried again, pushing hard, and heard metal groan, resisting him; then he scrambled over to the other side.

Fortunately, the back door had not been damaged, and he was able to lift out his wife. As he held her in his arms, her eyes opened.

"I feel so weak," she said. "And I am so cold."

"We'll have medical help soon," he told her.

An instant before the Rover exploded into flames, he managed to make it to the wooded area. Some embers fell against the leaves around the three of them and ignited these, which spread to the underbrush.

"West, Andrew!" Bartlett yelled. "There must be some houses to the west."

"But who can we trust, Dad?" the boy asked.

"We have no choice," his father pointed out.

The odor of smoke from the wrecked car and from the surrounding woods was becoming stronger. They moved as fast as they could. The ground was not a smooth highway but littered with overturned trees and slippery sections of leaves and mud.

Andrew tripped, fell, scrambled to his feet, and continued on.

More and more of the trees in back of them were in flames.

Bartlett's arms were beginning to ache, his vision blurring a bit, the smoke getting into his lungs.

"Dad, watch out!" Andrew yelled.

Bartlett had been heading straight for the trunk of a large tree directly in his path. He saw it in time and stepped around it.

Natalie started groaning.

"I'm so sick . . . . ," she muttered, her voice barely audible. "Oh, Stephen, I'm so very sick."

Suddenly her body went limp, and he thought, for a second, that she was dead.

Breathing.

He saw that she was breathing but also that her face had drained of color, and there were splotches of blood on her chin.

Oh, Lord, Lord, don't let it end like this for her, he prayed to himself. *Help us get through this madness.*

Though the fire was behind them and had not as yet caught up, a strong wind was blowing smoke in their direction, forcing it into their lungs.

Bartlett started coughing, his vision blurring even more than before.

Voices! People talking excitedly!

He tried to hold on, tried not to fall, but dizziness was overcoming him as well as exhaustion from all that had happened during the past hour and from the smoke in his lungs and . . . .

Bartlett was rapidly losing consciousness and felt Natalie slipping away from his grip—no, being *taken* from him. As he started to fall, strong hands caught him, and he heard his son's voice yelling something about answered prayer.

Bartlett felt a soft mattress beneath his body, a warm blanket on top of him. He reached out instinctively for his wife and found nothing.

His eyes shot open.

Sitting in a chair next to the bed was a thin, pale-faced woman in her mid-fifties, her hair already gray, dark circles prominent under her eyes. Thin lips moved into a smile as she saw that he had regained consciousness. She wiped her hands on the apron that covered her simple cotton housedress and felt his forehead for fever.

"They want you badly," she said. "But they shall not have you."

"My wife . . . my son," he mumbled, his strength mostly dissipated.

"They are no worse off than you are," she told him.

"But Natalie, she . . . she—"

"Your wife will survive. My husband is only what some might call a country doctor, but with the war before this one and with the horrors happening now he's had much experience with wounded bodies."

Her eyes became watery.

"Including his own," she said, her voice scarcely above a whisper.

"Your husband fought the Germans before?" Bartlett asked.

"He was a medic on the front lines from 1914 to 1916. A land mine exploded near him, and he was knocked unconscious. When he came to, he saw a German soldier standing over him with a bayonet aimed at his right leg. The soldier laughed maniacally and jabbed the bayonet into that leg again and again."

She was shaking with anger and revulsion.

"Cedric, my husband, had no weapon. Medics were supposed to be off-limits in those days, a nod to the so-called civility that was to have governed both sides."

"Military civility is a myth," Bartlett offered. "War invariably grinds it into the bloody earth."

"You are very right, young man. Cedric survived only because another soldier, a British one, saw what was happening and shot the German in the back. He then picked up my husband and carried him behind our lines. But as he was walking away from that spot, you know what Cedric kept babbling?"

"See if the German needs help . . . ."

"How did you know?" the woman asked, startled.

"I've met men like your husband before. They're a remarkable breed."

"His leg was saved but he walks with a limp, and there is much pain on damp days. We have many of those in this country I'm afraid."

Just then her husband entered the same room.

"I'm Cedric Gibbons," he said robustly. "I help you and the lad, and you end up flirting with my wife. Just like an American!"

He was chuckling as he said that. Barely shorter than Bartlett, who was over six feet tall and weighed two hundred-odd pounds, he approached the bed, grimacing a bit as he did so.

"For the rest of my life I will carry that man's hatred with me," he said, rubbing his hand slowly over the well-worn khaki trousers covering his thigh. Then, adjusting the suspenders over his plaid flannel shirt, he settled into a chair beside the bed.

"But you responded with concern for *his* welfare," Bartlett reminded Gibbons.

"A doctor *must* be dedicated to preserving life, not exacting vengeance. I hear my German counterparts routinely perform abortions to rid the world of non-Aryan babies. Any doctor who takes the life of an unborn child forfeits his right to practice a profession that is supposed to be a healing one. Thank God it is illegal in *this* country and elsewhere!"

"My wife, my son," Bartlett spoke, his voice growing a little stronger, "please tell me that they are safe."

"Indeed they are, I am happy to say," Gibbons remarked with some bravado. "I have been able to take out the bullet that was lodged in her chest. It missed hitting her heart and all other vital organs but caused some damage to an artery. She give up considerable blood, frankly, but I was able to stop any additional loss before it was too late. The lady is very weak, of course, but something quite miraculous has occurred, you know; I mean, it's a key reason why she's going to survive."

"Your quick action," Bartlett spoke, thinking he knew the answer.

"Not that. I do what I can. There is no miracle involved as such. *That* came when it turned out that I had her blood type in our village's blood bank. For some time now, we have been supplied with a limited supply as a precaution, should any of our flyers crash land in this vicinity or our men come ashore and not be able to make it in to London. Your wife's type is rather rare, but we had it available in a quantity that proved adequate."

"Andrew?" Bartlett asked.

"An amazing lad," Gibbons replied, admiration apparent on his face. "He actually participated as my assistant, handing me the right instruments when I needed each one. How could he have known?"

"I've tried to prepare him for certain eventualities. When London was under the blitz, I knew there was every chance that the building we were living in at the time could be hit. Andrew needed to be versed in whatever survival techniques he could handle, especially since I wasn't always home."

"I've already called in to London. The authorities seemed overjoyed when I told them you were here. You will have soldiers at your side as you all return. Very impressive, I must say. You seem to be a special sort of man."

Bartlett blushed at that.

"May I see Natalie and my son now?" he asked.

Gibbons nodded.

"Let me help you," he offered.

"Too much weight on your leg," Bartlett protested.

"My leg has been like this for nearly twenty years. I can handle anything, Stephen Bartlett."

"You know my name!"

"The boys at No. 10 Downing Street, including the Bulldog himself, are hardly strangers to me."

"Didn't mean to sound alarmed."

"I might have felt the same way if I had been through what you have."

Bartlett liked Cedric Gibbons but then he had also felt similarly about another individual a year earlier, and had been betrayed by the man.

Emil Kleist.

Kleist was supposed to have been his partner on a mission to bring about the assassination of Reinhard Heydrich, potentially the most dangerous of Hitler's henchmen because he was both brilliant and the least emotionally unstable, unlike the Führer himself. But it turned out that Kleist was in fact a double agent, and nearly succeeded in aborting the plan to kill the Butcher of Prague, which was Heydrich's infamous nickname.

The two men walked outside.

"A beautiful place to live," Bartlett remarked as he glanced at the small, quaint homes that looked as though they had been preserved from Elizabethan times.

"It has been wonderful here," Gibbons replied. "We're close enough to London that we can go in whenever we want but far enough away to be unaffected by the noise and the congestion. We have the antiquity without the more modern and highly undesirable ramifications of too many cars and too many people."

"That situation will only get worse," agreed Bartlett, "if there's anything left after the war."

"The blitz has stopped, yet you continue to sound pessimistic. Are you aware of something that I do not know?"

"Sabotage from the ground rather than destruction from the air. Hitler's plan is to so weaken Britain through the deeds of his undercover saboteurs that when Goering sends the Luftwaffe back in—"

"You think that is a possibility?" Gibbons interrupted, alarm on his face and in the tone of his voice. "The planes actually returning?"

"Oh, yes. Spies are flooding into the United States right as we speak. It is the same here, I regret to say. At least back home there is protection from the air. Goering has no fighter planes with enough range to reach us. So Himmler and his cronies are managing to infiltrate us with some of their best men, hoping to bring the U.S. to its knees through subversion."

"But England is within range of whatever they want to throw at us!"

Gibbons lost much of his former gregarious manner.

"I love the age of this nation," he muttered. "I love being in touch with what the centuries long gone have left behind. To see that turned to dust and pieces of rubble . . ."

He could not go on.

They were approaching a whitewashed building that was twice the size of any other in the village.

"On the first floor is what we call a village administration office, though there is little that requires other than the most routine attention," Gibbons assured him. "On the second are several beds and some decent medical equipment, none of which is used very much, but at least they remain there, available when we do need them. We are rather healthy out here, my friend, what with air that is clean, natural goods from nearby farmlands, and a quietude that is nothing short of a healing balm for one's nerves."

Gibbons opened the door and Bartlett walked past him.

Just in front of them, a cheerful, ruddy-faced woman in her early sixties looked up from a desk piled high with papers.

"This is Hillary Eaton," he said. "Hillary, meet Stephen Bartlett."

She stood with some effort, walked around the desk, and shook the American's hand with gusto.

"You have a wonderful family," she said. "Your wife came out of the anesthesia singing a hymn that was quite beautiful. Your son was holding her hand, and he joined in. I must admit that I cried."

Hillary led them upstairs.

Andrew saw his father immediately, jumped up, and rushed over to him.

"You're okay!" he yelled. "So is Mom!"

Natalie's eyes were open, and she smiled as Bartlett approached. He sat down on the left side of her bed, leaned over, and kissed her gently on the lips.

"I don't know how I could have gone on without you," he told her.

A moment later, the odor of burning wood and thatched hay rushed into that room from outside, along with the sound of people screaming.

Gibbons hurried to a window overlooking the village square. He saw half a dozen men with flamethrowers spraying the residences with fire. People he had known for many years were trying to escape but most, including women and children, were not able to do so, their bodies torched, several little toddlers crying in agony as their bodies hit the ground, writhing briefly and then becoming still.

"They've come after you, Stephen," he said with a mixture of terror and rage, coughing as smoke reached his lungs. "We're trapped I'm afraid."

Winston Churchill expected to be getting a different response than the one he received from his aide.

"An entire village burnt to a crisp?" He repeated the other man's words.

"That is what the report says," the aide went on in a deliberate monotone to conceal the emotion he still felt minutes after learning what had happened. "Men, women, and children—dead."

"Just like Lidice and that other town in Czechoslovakia."

"Virtually identical, sir."

"And the Bartletts?"

The aide dreaded having to give the answer that was the only accurate one.

"Nowhere to be found."

Churchill fell into momentary silence, rubbing his right hand across his thick, drooping lips.

"Sir?" the aide ventured.

"Yes, Hillerman?"

"They may be sent back to Germany, you know."

That thought hadn't occurred to Churchill. He assumed that any quest for vengeance by the Nazis would go only so far as a simple "execution," and that if successful, the attempt would leave behind three brutalized bodies. Period.

"We've contacted von Tresckow," Hillerman said.

"What does he suggest?"

"His behavior must be rather constrained for the moment."

"That *is* unfortunate," Churchill remarked.

"Quite, Sir. As you know, von Tresckow aroused some suspicion through his efforts to free Bartlett from imprisonment directly after the Heydrich assassination. He managed to concoct a story that he told the high command in Berlin: namely, that Stephen Bartlett was far more valuable alive than dead.

"Apparently, Lina Heydrich found out about this and raised what the Americans would call 'quite a ruckus.' By necessity, Henning von Tresckow now must lay low for a few months, which limits his actions not inconsiderably."

"He's no help at all then?"

"To the contrary, he had a very good suggestion, sir."

"What is it, Hillerman?"

"Rommel, sir. Erwin Rommel might be able to help. We are able to get in touch with the man through special, shall we say, 'intermediaries.'"

The Desert Fox!

Churchill's bloodshot eyes widened at the thought. Beads of perspiration appeared on his deeply lined forehead.

"We've known for some time of his dissatisfaction with Hitler's conduct of the war and his horror at the hints of barbarism coming out of the camps. But why in the world would he be helpful to *us* now?" the prime minister queried his aide.

"I suggest that it is because of his personal loathing for Reinhard Heydrich," Hillerman offered. "Rommel saw the man with the greatest clarity, as a monster who degraded everything he touched.

"Furthermore, since Rommel was so decisively d
Alamein and was forced to retreat, his physical conditi
has been at a very low ebb. He suffers from fainting spel
ach and intestinal complications, as well as an enlarged liver and cir-
culatory difficulties, intrinsically much like Himmler's condition,
according to what we have heard."

Churchill sucked in his breath, a slight twitch commencing at
his right cheek.

The aide knew how much the prime minister truly admired
Rommel and considered the German very much the equal of any of
the Allied generals. There were even some reports that Churchill had
become *obsessed* by a need to defeat the man because in doing so, he
could prove that even the best that Germany had to offer was not
able to stand against forces serving the cause of justice.

Churchill regained control and muttered, "Rommel is vulner-
able now. Is that what you are saying, Hillerman?"

The aide nodded quickly.

"Furthermore, you believe that he is in a unique position to act
without generating suspicion because, despite that singular defeat,
he remains Germany's most celebrated general. Some say their only
military hope."

"Precisely, sir," Hillerman assured the prime minister. "And
there is some possibility that if a coup or an assassination attempt
succeeds anytime over the coming months, Rommel may be the one
who is able to take charge of the government. Should that happen,
the man will undoubtedly *not* prolong the war another day. He is
said to be in favor of putting Hitler and the other Nazis on trial for
their crimes."

Churchill was glad to be reminded of this but knew that any
such developments were still in the future, while the safety of the
Bartlett family was an immediate concern.

"But, I wonder, will this Rommel," the prime minister spoke in
his most deliberate and portentous manner, "who is known to vac-
illate from time to time once he has left the battlefield, prove to be
quite courageous enough to stand up to the powerful mastermind
behind this brutal assault on Stephen and his loved ones?"

"Are you speaking of Heinrich Himmler, sir?" the aide inquired.

"You guess correctly," Churchill assured him. "Is there any reason to believe that Rommel will have the resolve needed for this task?"

Hillerman grimaced as he replied, "We can only hope and pray
that he does."

3

Stephen Bartlett regained consciousness only to lose it in numerous shifting waves, flashes of sight and sound reaching him . . . being loaded onto what seemed to be a boat, then the sounds of an engine chugging . . . transferal, then, to another boat quite different from the first, followed by the sensation of going down, down . . .

An Unterseeboot!

A U-boat, the German version of a submarine.

Initially the American could not tell whether Natalie and Andrew had been taken along with him or had been sent elsewhere. Any periods of being alert, and it was an exaggeration in itself to call them that, lasted only seconds at a time, amounting to mere smatterings of faces, a quick glimpse of a periscope, narrow corridors, all blending together to form a haphazard and disconcerting collage.

Every time he tried to reach out, to pull himself from an encompassing abyss, strong hands seemed to fold around his arms, his legs, and push him back into oblivion despite his cries, his words that floated somehow to the surface of his consciousness, "My wife, my son, don't hurt them, please, please don't . . ."

His pleas brought coarse laughter, sometimes a stinging slap across the cheek. Once, as he happened to overhear a rambling conversation, he caught in the midst of it a particular name, a woman's name . . . Lina!

That one sent him back into darkness, screaming.

Land.

In what seemed to be the early-morning hours, Bartlett knew that he had been shifted from a sea-going vessel to a land vehicle, although he still could not make that final leap from engulfing darkness to full awareness of his surroundings. Once, he cried out again for his wife, his son, but there was no reply from either of them.

A bumpy road.

He was being driven over a bumpy road, every rut translating into pain for his already abused body.

As an indeterminate amount of time passed, he sensed feeling returning to his body; sounds became more distinct, continuous, and odors became apparent: sweat, tobacco, leather, a certain mustiness.

Finally Bartlett opened his eyes with great caution, trying not to attract any attention, and saw, after they had adjusted sufficiently to the light, that he was in the back of a very old Mercedes, the padding in the seats slipping through cracked and split sections of red leather. He was handcuffed, but there were no restraints on his legs. A Gestapo agent in a trademark black trench coat was sitting to his left, and in the front seat were two others, one of them driving the car.

They've decided to split us up, he surmised. *Any rescue now will be that much more difficult.*

Bartlett knew he had to try to escape before they reached whatever their destination was. Being locked in a basement somewhere, possibly chained to a stone wall, meant far fewer possibilities for getting away.

Just after the assassination of Reinhard Heydrich, he had been captured and confined to a similar place because of his participation in the successful plot to kill the man adored by the Nazis but viewed by the rest of the world as one of the most vile and hate-filled henchmen serving the Führer. It was only the intervention of dissident general Henning von Tresckow that got Bartlett out of the prison, though he was later recaptured.

And the wolves, he remembered, *especially Vulf.*

But neither his wild canine friends or von Tresckow could help him now. He had to escape entirely on his own, and the only way he could do that seemed to be through causing commotion sufficient to allow him to swing open the back door of the Mercedes, roll out without injuring himself badly, and run off into the woods.

The Gestapo agent next to him was sleepy, his head bobbing a bit. Those in the front seat were intent on the road ahead of them.

Bartlett judged that he could kick the one agent in the jaw, possibly breaking it, and then immediately grab the interior door handle, lift it up, and be outside in an instant before anyone could act to stop him.

One thing was clear: He had no other option.

He braced himself against the door, and in a karate-like kick, jammed the heels of his feet against the Gestapo agent's neck and jaw. He succeeded, the man screaming in pain as his jaw fractured. Then Bartlett lifted himself up and grabbed for the metal door handle, his sprained fingers closing painfully around it.

A split second later, he tumbled out onto the road, which hugged the side of a mountain to his right. To his left, the road ended at the edge of a drop of thousands of feet to a bucolic-looking valley below.

No woods.

Nothing to run toward. No place whatever to hide.

By now the two uninjured Gestapo agents were out of the Mercedes and standing in front of him, smiling.

"Nowhere to run?" one of them sneered.

"You hurt our comrade," the other one said. "Now we hurt you."

They walked very slowly toward him. When they were less than a couple of feet away, Bartlett dropped onto his back and kicked upward at the two of them. Both were knocked over, expressions of surprise distorting their faces.

He started running down the road, hoping a wooded area was somewhere ahead.

Suddenly one of the agents sprang to his feet and lunged after him, leaving his moaning partner still on the ground.

He grabbed Bartlett around the neck and started choking him.

"We were supposed to bring you to the castle *alive* if at all possible," he growled. "It no longer is."

The road was narrow.

Bartlett staggered toward the edge, the agent holding on to him, the hold tightening, cutting off his oxygen.

He could see movement to one side. The man whose jaw he had broken was staggering out of the Mercedes, a Luger in one hand.

Bartlett turned himself deliberately in that direction. The injured Gestapo agent raised the pistol, aimed it.

Instantly Bartlett swung around as a shot was fired.

His attacker's eyes widened in shock and pain. Staggering forward, he gripped his neck as blood seeped between his fingers.

Enraged, the agent with the Luger started firing wildly.

One bullet grazed the top of Bartlett's shoulder, tearing the padded jacket he had been wearing but not making contact with his flesh. Nevertheless, he stumbled backward toward the edge of the road, and then over, a single scream tearing past his lips.

Trembling a bit, Lina Heydrich replaced the receiver on its ancient black cradle. She could scarcely control her emotions as she repeated in her mind the words that had just been spoken to her.

Stephen Bartlett has been captured!

The American was now being transported to a mountaintop castle at the eastern edge of the Bavarian Alps, only a short distance from where she had been staying since she left Czechoslovakia. The informant had told her to wait for a second phone call that would inform her as to when she should leave.

Less than an hour away, she thought. *Soon I will be able to look at him, spit in his face, and then watch as he is tortured until he dies.*

And his family.

The woman and child were being taken elsewhere, as originally planned, just in case the Allies had in mind any sudden rescue attempt, cutting down the odds that Bartlett *and* his loved ones both would be saved.

What will I do with his woman and his son? she asked herself coldly. *Perhaps I will decide to turn this Natalie Bartlett into a common whore to satiate the appetites of randy SS officers. Yes, that would be a good fate for her. As for the boy, though Himmler hates to acknowledge it, there are those in his ranks as well as within the Gestapo who would find the eight-year-old an attractive companion for a time.*

She thought of her own children, thought of the life they now would have to lead without the extraordinary father they loved so much, thought of the baby lost in her miscarriage after her husband's murder.

"I will try to be everything he was, dearest ones," she whispered to the surrounding emptiness of the room in that rented house, so barren of memories after all those that had surrounded her in their estate just outside Prague. "I will raise you to hate the Jew garbage your father found so loathsome, to kill them whenever you can and in the worst possible ways, ways that prolong their agony."

Her gaze rested on the photograph in its hand-carved wooden frame on the desk behind which she sat.

"My love . . . ," she said with great tenderness.

The phone rang.

Her hand reached out for it in an instant.

"Yes . . . ," she said, somewhat nervously, hoping that whoever it was had no bad news for her, for if she were told that Bartlett had escaped—

"The American tried to run," the voice at the other end stated.

"Did he succeed?" she asked, her voice stone cold.

"No, he did not."

She listened to the rest of the information, and then slammed down the receiver, hurting her hand slightly in the process.

"Good!" she proclaimed, her face flushed red with excitement.

Stephen Bartlett was fired at minutes ago by a member of the Gestapo, and now the American has fallen over . . .

Clasping her hands together, she tried to stop her entire body from shaking with anticipation.

My mind must be absolutely clear, she thought. *My aim must be sure. I cannot waste a single shot.*

And then Lina Heydrich, the still-grieving widow of the Butcher of Prague, a man once considered to be a probable successor to Adolf Hitler himself, raced from that room to the rendezvous that had been promised.

4

Stephen Bartlett's fall to the valley below was broken by an outjutting ledge, which seemed to move somewhat as his body hit it, stirring up dusty soil that probably had not been otherwise disturbed for a very long time.

Voices.

Directly above him.

Bartlett glanced up the twenty feet or so, and saw the Gestapo agent who had shot him bending over the edge of the road, aiming the Luger.

Jammed.

The pistol jammed.

I wonder if there are any truly reliable handguns these days, Bartlett thought, grateful that the weapon could not be fired, but also remembering that a Sten submachine gun aimed at Reinhard Heydrich also had jammed, complicating the job of assassinating him.

The agent backed away, and Bartlett turned his attention to the ledge.

It was less than seven feet square.

The impact of his body had loosened it considerably from the mountainside. As he tried to stand, it wobbled under him.

Bartlett turned and glanced over the edge. Another thirty feet or so below, he saw a second ledge that was still a long distance from the valley floor. Even if he came upon a series of such ledges, it was likely that the Gestapo would be waiting for him by the time he reached the ground, wasting any effort he put into the descent.

He couldn't climb back to the road and he couldn't continue down!

It seemed that he had nothing left to do but just wait there, wait for more Gestapo agents to be sent for and, finally, arrive.

Still standing, but feeling a bit dizzy, he braced himself against the side of the mountain, tilting his head upward, and saw the clear sky. Several large, hawk-like birds were flying overhead. In the distance he heard the sound of timber wolves.

Wolves!

For a moment Bartlett's mind flashed back to the night a year earlier when a wolf he had befriended chose later to repay him by seemingly organizing other wolves and attacking the group of Nazi soldiers who had been assigned the task of executing him, along with a small group of German Resistance members.

Vulf . . . he thought with real tenderness of the animal's name again. *Without you, I would never have seen my family again.*

But Vulf was gone. And the distant sound of a pack of wolves no longer meant the possibility of rescue.

A gunshot rang out in the quiet of that isolated spot.

One of the birds started behaving like a plane hit by anti-aircraft fire.

It plummeted from where it had been flying and headed down the mountainside, bounced off a large, outjutting boulder, then continued toward the valley below.

Laughter.

One of the agents had gotten his kicks for the day!

Something quite startling happened a second or two later.

The other birds, half a dozen of them, swooped down on the road.

Unlike other, more timid species that would have simply flown away without hesitation, spooked by the incident, these were apparently very aggressive predators who reacted altogether differently.

More shots were fired.

He heard cries of pain, a man screaming in agony, more bullets fired.

Minutes later, five of the birds took to the air again, ignoring Bartlett completely.

Bartlett waited, listening for the slightest indication of any kind of movement on the road above him.

Ten more minutes passed.

Still nothing . . .

Bartlett surveyed the distance between him and the road.

The mountain was not a smooth wall of rock. There seemed to be many spots for his hands and his feet.

He dug into the side, testing for loose soil and rocks. The section just above his head seemed quite firm.

He pulled himself up.

As soon as he did, the ledge, having been loosened by the impact of his weight hitting it and now suddenly relieved of it, tore away from the mountainside and broke into uncountable pieces as it began its descent.

Bartlett let out his breath in quick spurts, wondering how much longer his weight would have been tolerated.

He pulled himself up the side slowly, his muscular arms and legs providing the strength he needed.

When Bartlett finally reached the top, he looked with special caution over the edge at the road.

Three bodies.

One of these had already been dead when the predators attacked.

The other two lay crumpled on the ground not far from him, little left of their faces after the birds had hacked away at them.

Bartlett was about to climb over when he heard the intruding sound of an automobile that seemed to be only a short distance away. He turned and saw it coming up the winding, sloping road.

As he started to scamper back down the mountainside, he heard a woman's shrill voice screaming, "That's him! That's the American. *Get him!*"

Tires squealed as brakes were slammed. After jumping out of the car, two Gestapo agents came running toward him, pistols in hand.

He had only a few seconds and no weapons, no—

To his left was a fist-sized rock stuck into the side of the mountain. While maintaining a hold with his right hand, he reached out with his left, closing his fingers around the rock and pulling on it in one quick move.

Loose.

It was quite loose and came away without much effort.

Footsteps, heels grinding dirt on that primitive road. Men sucking in their breath as they approached.

The sun was to their backs. The closer they got to him, the more pronounced their shadows. He could tell approximately the position of each one.

Bartlett knew that he had to swing the rock with uncommon accuracy, hit the agent to his left and, virtually at the same time, jump onto the road, making contact with the other man before he could fire his pistol with any accuracy.

Closer.

They seemed to be nearly at the road's edge.

Bartlett acted, letting the rock go with all the force he could manage. In the next instant, while he sprang over, he heard one of the men groan. The other's eyes widened as he saw the hefty American barrel into him.

The two men struggled on the ground, Bartlett hammering away at the Nazi with both fists . . . first, the left . . . then, the right . . . then both at the same time.

He thought he heard footsteps in back of him but he couldn't divert his attention to find out for sure.

A voice.

Strangely familiar.

A woman's voice.

"I shall be quite happy to blow the top of your head off right now if you do not stop immediately," whoever it was ordered him. "Give me that pleasure, I beg you. Do continue resisting, please!"

He froze, recognizing it now.

"Stand, Stephen Bartlett," the voice commanded. "Stand and face me, with your hands raised above your head."

He released the Gestapo agent, got to his feet, and turned slowly in the direction of the speaker.

"It has been nearly a year," Lina Heydrich said, a crooked smile on her pale, vein-lined, no longer beautiful face. "I am very pleased to be able to meet you again."

She laughed hoarsely, a deep frown on her forehead.

"I suspect, though, that you do not share my feelings about this moment," she added. "Nor will your wife and son when they are delivered to me elsewhere."

5

Little light came into the room from any source except a narrow opening in the upper part of one wall and from under the door.

Stephen Bartlett was in otherwise complete darkness. And he had no doubt that this was part of his "punishment."

Odors.

Musty, damp.

There was a sense of the ancient in the very air.

He caught glimpses of the castle as they approached it.

This time Bartlett's legs also were cuffed. He had been able to see his destination only for a second or two at a time, when the car had swung around a curve and the massive old structure was visible.

It had seemed indeed very much a well-preserved medieval fortress on a massive scale, located at the very top of that mountain peak, built when airplanes were not a potential vehicle of attack. On the ground, though, it appeared to be totally protected from any attempt at rescue of its prisoners from an outside assault.

"You will die here!" Lina Heydrich announced as she sat in the front seat. "You have no hope now, Stephen Bartlett. No one knows where you are. You are beyond redemption. I know how familiar you Christians are with that word. But a future life will not help you now, nor will the God of the *Juden!*"

"My wife, my son," Bartlett blurted. "Where are they? Why them? They're innocent. They did nothing to your husband."

A smirk appeared on her face.

"Sometimes justice takes all before it," she said.

"Where is the justice in this?"

"Nazi justice, Stephen Bartlett. Like no other in the world!"

Then he was hurried down to what must have been the dungeon area and thrown in the encompassing darkness.

It might be, he knew, that his captors would try to crack his sanity by the isolation they were forcing upon him in that dreary room, if room were the apt word at all, keeping him where he could see little, where he could only hear and smell. Even after what must have been several hours, his eyes could pick up so little, the faintest indication that the room had been carved out of the bare rock of that mountain, with the castle built over it, and possibly only a narrow tunnel leading from one to the other.

Hear and smell . . .

Hear the dripping of water.

Hear scratching sounds. Movement of some kind.

Smell something putrid, close to him.

And see . . .

So faintly that it might have been a trick of the mind, of the senses, deprived as they were of so much to which they had become accustomed.

In the darkness the hint of shapes.

At first he thought of rats.

He had never been scared of these, for they touched no inner corner of madness within him. Indeed, he had had rats as pets years before.

They're miscalculating already, he thought, *if they think I'm susceptible to this kind of mind game.*

Not rats.

What he finally perceived in that abyss-like place of confinement was not the movement of rats at all.

Something else.

A wild guess, he surmised. *They couldn't have known. It's not recorded in any file that a double agent could have perused.*

No, that was not a real fear of his, not rats, but instead something quite different, something from almost primeval depths that caused his nerves to—

Spiders.

He saw their vague shapes, saw the webs they had spun into one corner of the room, saw them crawling along the walls and the floor.

Toward him.

Drawn by his scent or the warmth of his body or whatever it was.

Still on his feet, he backed away, in a corner.

They kept coming.

One of the spiders, large, black, its thorax oblong in shape, with fuzz so thick it almost looked like fur on the back of its long, bent legs, climbed onto his bare foot. He shook it off, using his heel to squash it.

Others followed but he was able, temporarily, to stay away from them by stumbling to another corner.

He felt something faintly sticky at his ear.

Another web.

He had backed into it.

Something was on top of his head, moving about in his hair.

He raised one hand to brush it off.

It jumped onto the back of that hand.

A very large spider.

It seemed to hesitate, as though studying him, then started to crawl up his arm. He stood, transfixed, paralyzed, unable to move or scream.

On his shoulder now.

Toward his cheek.

And then his mouth.

Its legs searching between his lips for an opening, tickling his lips as it probed.

Finally, Stephen Bartlett screamed, and as he did, the spider grabbed the opportunity, and scampered into his mouth. He could feel it touching the surface of his tongue and apparently heading toward his throat.

He retched, coughing up the creature, along with everything that was left in his stomach, his body bent over, the room and its darkness spinning around.

Abruptly, the door was flung open.

Strong hands grabbed him, and he was pulled from the room.

He was covered with perspiration.

Lina Heydrich stood beside a massive, black-shirted SS trooper.

Behind Bartlett, holding his arms in a painful grip, was another trooper, equally tough-looking.

"Disgusting," she said, smiling. "You've made a mess of yourself. Have you Americans no sense of proper hygiene?"

"My wife, my son," Bartlett groaned.

"We can only hope they will be alive long enough for Mengele to have some real fun with them," she replied, relishing that revelation.

Mengele! Rumored to be the most maniacal of Hitler's "biological pioneers," and recently appointed chief doctor at Auschwitz. I've heard that the commandants of other camps are eager to have him, to learn from him!

Bartlett tried to pull away from the trooper holding him.

"You are a big man," observed the widow of the Butcher of Prague. "But you have become weak. And you are quite doomed, you know that, do you not?"

"Like the tens of thousands of innocent people your husband planned to murder?" Bartlett spat out the words. "This is the man you want to avenge with crimes of your own—a mass murderer without conscience?"

She slapped him hard across the cheek.

"You dare not speak of him in that way!" she said.

"What other way is there?" he persisted, more than a little recklessly. "As a devoted husband? Is that it? You think you have been the only woman to share his bed during the years of his marriage? Is that what you believe?"

"I believe the truth," she said, nearly screaming. "I do not accept as fact the ugliness that others say, only what I know."

"So you admit the rumors then?"

She turned away, but not before he could see the redness in her cheeks, the beads of perspiration on her forehead.

"You can ignore the women, perhaps. Yes, you might be able to do that; but what about the men?" Bartlett continued recklessly, letting his anger and contempt dominate him. "What about those handsome *Jewish* men?"

She swung around on one heel and hit him in the groin with her fist.

"Liar!" Lina Heydrich said at the top of her voice. "Vulgar rumors perpetrated by non-Aryan scum."

Bartlett was doubled over, barely able to speak.

"Even . . . if you are . . . correct," he muttered painfully, "shouldn't these people use . . . whatever weapons . . . they . . . have . . . to . . . try and destroy . . . your husband . . . any way they can? After all . . . he . . . and others like him have taken away everything they have! How . . . can you . . . expect them to . . . stand . . . by and do . . . nothing?"

"But my children," she rebutted, "my children have suffered."

"How many *children* are ending up in those efficient new ovens over which your husband seemed so eager to preside?" Bartlett said, the pain subsiding enough to enable him to speak more firmly.

"Jew babies!" Lina Heydrich said, her eyes wide and wild-looking. "Aryan children are pure. They have not a single drop of contemptible Jew blood in them. Garbage is *supposed* to be incinerated, is it not?"

"Wrong! Reinhard Heydrich found out that he had a cousin in Dusseldorf who was Jewish," Bartlett said, hardly able to mask his delight in revealing this to her. "He never let anyone know about this. After he uncovered the truth, your husband went so far as to personally murder the poor woman only a few months before his own death. He put a gun to the back of her head and blew her brains out!"

Lina raised her hand to slap him again, disbelief registering on her face.

"It's true, you know," he said, his voice as emotionless as he could manage to keep it. "Your precious Aryan offspring come from a lineage that *is* part Jewish!"

"*Shoot him!*" she ordered. "Take him outside in the courtyard right this minute and shoot the American now!"

The SS trooper beside her smiled crookedly.

"Here is my Luger," he said. "Why do you not reserve that pleasure for yourself? As an act of tribute to your husband as well as your children?"

She held the gun, a pale tongue darting out between her lips.

"It could have been otherwise, you know," she said, looking at Bartlett, for some instance a fleeting expression of regret playing across her face. "We could have had an interesting time, you and I, especially if you had lingered in the big bedroom for even a little while after searching through it."

She was referring to the only previous time she had met the American . . . the day her husband died. With everyone's attention distracted by the assassination attempt several miles away, Bartlett had donned the black-leather garb of a Gestapo agent and, using counterfeit identification, had made his way into the luxurious castle-like house the Nazis had provided for their dynamic "hero" and his family.

"*May I ask if you are part-Swedish?*" *he had inquired as she invited him inside, impressed by her fresh, blonde-haired beauty.*

"*Quite so, Mr.—,*" *she replied, fumbling with his name, which she had already forgotten.*

"*Brimmer, Frau Heydrich, Hans Brimmer. I suspect my diction is not what it used to be,*" *he said pleasantly, taking away her momentary embarrassment.* "*Interrogating too many Jews perhaps.*"

She found that amusing, as he had intended.

"You are very . . . large," she said.

"But your husband is tall, is he not?"

"To a midget, yes!" she said, trying some humor of her own.

Bartlett chuckled politely.

"I meant," she continued, "that you are broad, muscular. So many of the Gestapo look like little weasels."

"There are many who would agree with you."

She looked at him intently for a moment.

"You seem so . . . so—," she said, fumbling her thought.

"Young?"

"Yes, yes, that's it! I wasn't sure that you are so young as you appear."

"I am not."

"What is your age?"

"Must I?"

"If I tell mine, will you tell yours?"

"Surely, Frau Heydrich."

"Well, I'm not going to do so!"

She smiled broadly at that.

Bartlett found her personality to be the opposite of his perceptions. He never expected someone with such a lighthearted, rather flirtatious manner.

"Have you been driving long?" she asked.

"I am afraid that that is the case."

"May I get you some tea?"

"I have something to tell you, Frau Heydrich."

"Has . . . has something happened to my husband?" she blurted out, then realized that he would not have been so conversational if that were the reason for his visit. She added, "Sorry to be so apprehensive. You see, Reinhard and I are still very much in love even after all these years."

She spoke as someone who understood the need to keep up appearances, at least to a degree, and her remark fit squarely into that category.

"I would like to check over this beautiful house for—," he started to say.

"A bomb?" she asked. "Do you think—?"

"Not that," he assured her.

She was greatly relieved.

"Termites perhaps?" she said mischievously.

"We would have sent a guard from Auschwitz for that purpose," he said, finding it difficult to be facetious.

She threw her head back and roared with laughter.

"Listening devices," he added. *"Sometimes they can be quite small and hard to uncover."*

"Go anywhere you like," she assured him. *"Our house is yours. Perhaps you will find one in the big bedroom. Bedrooms are logical places, I understand."*

"Indeed they are," he agreed.

Bartlett remembered the scene nearly as well as she had. How could he have forgotten? Lina Heydrich was undeniably attractive, with her shoulder-length blonde hair, her ample figure, that demeanor of a fashion model that she wore a bit obviously perhaps, but also enticingly, coupled with the mischievous manner with which she confronted him, her body language sending a message that was unmistakable.

But how different the passage of months had made her!

Now so pale, so much older looking . . .

Dark circles hung glaringly under her eyes, a permanent frown creased what had been a porcelain-smooth forehead, and her eyes were constantly red-rimmed. Instead of the overt seductiveness that had characterized her the year before, she was possessed of a hardness now, a brutal manner that was not unlike what had been true of Reinhard Heydrich himself.

She truly loved a monster, he thought.

Lina Heydrich reached out, touching his right cheek with her finger.

"You must be Aryan," she said, nearly whispering. "You have such strong features, such good skin. Your blue eyes seem—"

She leaned forward, pressing her mouth against his, her tongue finding its way between his lips.

Then she pulled back suddenly.

"Now!" she ordered, wiping her lips with the back of her hand. "We take care of this assassin now!"

Bartlett was dragged along a centuries-old corridor and up a flight of stairs that had been chiseled out of solid rock. Then one of the troopers flung open a heavy wooden door and Bartlett was pushed outside, into the castle's courtyard.

Confronting him, flanked by half a dozen armed soldiers, was a short, stocky but wiry man dressed in official military garb with plentiful medals and insignia.

"Frau Heydrich, what are you planning to do with that Luger I see in your hand?" Field Marshal Erwin Rommel spoke slowly, his tone icy. "The American has been transferred into my custody. I suggest that you put it away."

6

For some little while, Rommel sat impassively in the back seat of his Mercedes, which was being followed by a military vehicle carrying the soldiers he had brought with him. Driving the car was the personal assistant he had had since before World War II had started, Lieutenant Peter Hochberg, a man who was considerably taller than his boss, with large cheekbones, a broad, rather flattened nose, and thick lips.

This contrasted with Rommel's own physical stature and his strong but pale features, which could have caused people upon first meeting to ignore him altogether, though no one who knew about his accomplishments ever made that mistake.

His eyes, Stephen Bartlett thought as he sat beside the silent Rommel. *They are as commanding as any I have ever seen.*

The ride had gone just a bit more than twenty miles from the castle when the American finally and somewhat tentatively spoke.

"How . . . did you find out about me and where I was being held?" he asked.

"I have certain contacts who keep open certain channels of communication," Rommel spoke with slightly exaggerated evasiveness.

"But what reason do you have to do anything for me?"

Rommel grunted at what he considered the other man's rather impertinent manner.

"I can see that the woman is quite deranged by her grief," he observed, without answering directly. "I find that rather understandable, frankly."

Strangely, Bartlett felt somewhat intimidated as well as annoyed by such a man. Of all the generals in the German Army, Rommel was the most feared and the most respected by the Allies, the latter coming from appreciation of his tactical skills but also from the way he treated Allied prisoners, insisting that they be fed with the same food given to his own troops. Any uncovered brutality by one or more of his men against a prisoner was greeted with punishment under direct orders of the field marshal himself.

Bartlett waited a moment or two before speaking again, sensing that he should pull back a bit.

"Pardon me, sir, but regarding Lina Heydrich, there *is* something else, isn't there?" he ventured, though admittedly with a greater degree of nervousness than he had felt a moment earlier.

"You are correct," Rommel admitted without hesitating. "What I am failing to grasp is how such a monster as her husband could have inspired such a woman."

Bartlett was surprised by that sudden admission of what Rommel thought of Reinhard Heydrich.

"But others seem to think of him as a hero," the American ventured.

"Only the Nazis are capable of that, Stephen Bartlett. Anyone who is the least bit rational knew that Heydrich was loathsome."

"And Nazis are never rational?"

"If they were, they would not *be* Nazis in the first place."

"Yet Frau Heydrich seemed reasonably well-balanced when we first met, if rather flirtatious."

Rommel turned abruptly in the American's direction.

"What were the circumstances?" he demanded sharply, a look of instant suspicion on his face.

Bartlett told him.

"One cannot blame her for being flirtatious," Rommel added, satisfied by that response. "Her husband had beds reserved for him all over the Fatherland! The stories of his caprices are, shall we say, legends of a sort."

"But why her seeming devotion posthumously?"

"Guilt. Unlike the man himself, she is capable of basic human feelings."

Bartlett nodded in agreement.

"I can see that now," he said.

"But guilt can make anyone dangerous," Rommel said. "It tends to drive those who suffer from it to desperate acts, including vengeance against the innocent."

He paused for only seconds, then acknowledged, "You see, I know of this because I have some guilt of my own."

"About the government you serve?" Bartlett suggested, wondering if he would regret doing so.

"Precisely. About the hundreds of thousands of people dying in the camps. About going on with a war that is already lost, its continuance costing the lives of countless numbers of brave men on both sides."

Rommel turned away.

"And, also, about the young and impressionable ones being corrupted by Nazi dogma," he added.

"Through the Hitler Youth organizations?"

"Yes . . . it would have been far different if I had been in charge."

Bartlett had heard the stories. Rommel had been in line for the job. But a Nazi zealot named Baldur von Schirach took over instead.

"The man sought to militarize them," Rommel remarked. "I wanted to stress their education and the development of their character. Because of him and the successors that followed, they became little Napoleons instead of Einsteins."

"But, sir, you've had no part whatsoever in any of this: the camps, the corruption of the youth groups or even the war's going on. You wanted the carnage to be stopped months ago."

"My guilt lies not in the matter of never having tried, for I surely have done that with the greatest possible zeal and, I hope, intelligence, but, rather, having done my best, I nevertheless have failed."

He cleared his throat.

"And because of that failure, however gallant it might be," he went on, "there are now additional bodies being piled higher and higher on the battlefields of a ravaged Europe and in the pitiable ditches around Auschwitz, Birkenau, Treblinka, Dachau, and a dozen or more other places of great horror, so great in fact that even a cold-hearted devil such as Eichmann was appalled when he visited a few."

Rommel slammed a fist down on the back seat, his anger almost palpable.

"The Germany of great art and music, of the finest intellect, the Germany of Martin Luther and the Reformation, is now nothing more than an asylum of insane butchers running wild in the streets!

"I love this nation of mine. And I can hardly contain my agony as I see it being raped daily, victimized by the excesses of a gang of deranged egomaniacs. My abiding fear is that this beloved

Deutschland of my birth, for which I would give my life, will be laid waste by its enemies before the madmen responsible are driven from their seats of power."

The Desert Fox fell silent, consumed by his regrets.

Lina Heydrich had just finished talking with Heinrich Himmler. She could not stop trembling with anger as she put the phone receiver back on its cradle.

You promised to support me, she thought, her lips curled up into a snarl. *You agreed that my husband needed to be avenged. That is why you ordered without delay the destruction of those two villages. And yet now the death of a single man, a despicable American—indeed, one of the chief perpetrators of Reinhard's death—somehow seems to trouble you because this Rommel has become involved. You said he must have a reason and until you talk to him you cannot agree to any more activity.*

"You are little more than a traitor like the others," she had bellowed rashly into the receiver, realizing a second afterward that no one normally ever talked to Himmler in that manner, no matter what the circumstances were.

Click.

He had broken the connection without responding to that last invective.

Behind her anger was a sense of frustration.

For the years of her marriage to Reinhard Heydrich, Lina Heydrich had stood in the almost palpable shadow of his manifold ambitions as well as the dominating personality that gave rise to them.

But she also saw what he was successful in hiding from outsiders, instances of insecurity that would reveal themselves at odd moments, surfacing occasionally when he tried to make love to her and was unable to do so. He would retreat from her for days afterward but always she would entice him back into bed, and inevitably lovemaking proved to be no problem the next time.

Your hips, Lina recalled, with the slightest of smiles forming on her lips. *They were fatter than a man's normally would have been, more like a woman's actually. I knew this bothered you, though you never once admitted it to me. How many times did I catch you standing in front of a mirror, looking at yourself?*

She brought both hands to her mouth.

I miss you so much, she thought. *I miss your strength. Yet I know I have to survive on my own, raise our children so that they can be sent out to serve the glory of Deutschland as you did so well, my love.*

Stephen Bartlett.

Lina wiped away the tears that were beginning to form as she thought yet again of the American.

"You took everything away from me except my children!" she said, not realizing that she had begun to speak loudly. "There was so much that we all had to look forward to after Germany won the war."

A knock at the door.

She did not hear it.

"This very moment, Stephen Bartlett, your wife and your son are entering the gates of Dachau," she went on. "Josef Mengele is quite willing to heed my pleas even as Himmler fails to do so. He is set to visit Dachau while he is away from Auschwitz for a few days. He said it was his pleasure to accommodate me."

A Gestapo agent, the one who earlier had handed her the Luger, entered.

"I heard your voice, Frau Heydrich," he commented. "You were shouting."

She snapped her head in his direction.

"I want the American," she insisted.

"But Rommel is—," the agent started to say.

"Then they both have to be taken care of!"

"You cannot comprehend what you are asking for, Frau Heydrich. Field Marshal Rommel is the most respected military figure we have."

"If you will not help me, I will hire the assassins myself."

"The American's family has been assigned to Mengele. Is that not enough?"

She stood and strode over to the agent, slapping him across the cheek.

"It is *not!*" she declared. "There must be *nothing* left of them. That includes Stephen Bartlett himself. *See to it!*"

He nodded and left the room, closing the door behind him.

She is asking the impossible, he told himself as he hurried to a phone in another room down a musty-smelling corridor in that cold, damp ancient castle. *I cannot bypass my superiors, no matter how much I admired Reinhard Heydrich.*

Finding a scratched and rusty old phone in another bedroom, the Gestapo agent quickly dialed Berlin and waited nervously for the connection to Heinrich Himmler's office.

Felix Kellar could not believe what he was hearing from the widow of Reinhard Heydrich. He had been involved in espionage for a long time and had been privy to a host of attempted assassinations, sabotage, and other undercover operations extending back to World War I, and he was not prone to being startled by anything. But what the woman was asking of him seemed utterly bizarre and took even him by surprise.

"Assassinate Erwin Rommel!" he exclaimed into the phone receiver. "You *are* joking, of course, Frau Heydrich? Are you not?"

Silence.

She said nothing for a moment, then went on: "I am *not* joking, Herr Kellar. Your *real* purpose is to be that of exterminating the American. Field Marshal Rommel's death is only a cover for the rest."

. . . only a cover.

Kellar repeated those words only in his mind, thinking of how cold, how merciless they seemed even to him—brutal, unfeeling acts almost beyond his personal experience.

The greatest German military mind of the century killed as mere camouflage!

Lina Heydrich must have sensed his reluctance.

"My husband saved the life of your son," she reminded him. "You said, in return, that he could have your soul if he wanted it."

Kellar's thin, almost feminine fingers tapped a rhythm on top of the desk in front of him, for he had always suspected that that declaration would come back to haunt him, however much he had meant it at the time.

"Yes, yes," he assured her. "I did tell him that."

"I am calling in your debt now," Lina spoke firmly.

"I understand that; yes, I understand that."

"Will you do it for me, for Reinhard?"

Kellar knew he could scarcely refuse. And yet the danger needed to be impressed upon this woman.

"It will be a monstrous task," he told her. "And it will be very expensive."

"I have the money," she replied. "The cost is not important. Only the success of the operation is."

"What is your time frame, Frau Heydrich?"

"Today is Monday. It must be completed by Friday."

Kellar dropped the receiver when he heard that.

After apologizing, he quickly remarked, "We need weeks, Frau Heydrich. This is not some minor official, you know. It would not be a great deal more complicated if you wanted the Führer himself dead!"

"By Friday," Lina repeated, no emotion of any kind apparent in her voice. "I know where Rommel and the American are going to be. Take whatever number of men you judge necessary, and do it."

"Frontal attack is not the way," Kellar mused. "The Field Marshal has men guarding him all the time. It would have to be explosives."

"Excellent. My husband died from explosives. So shall Stephen Bartlett and anyone guarding him."

"At night," Kellar added. "The devices will be well-hidden, to be set off from a safe distance. My men can go in afterward, pretend to be rescuers, and shoot anyone who happens to be left alive."

"Excellent. I wasn't wrong to place my confidence in you."

"At what location do you want to be notified?"

"I will be at Dachau. Contact me in the commandant's office."

"Dachau? Why Dachau, Frau Heydrich, if I may ask?"

"I have plans for the wife and the son of Stephen Bartlett."

"I do not understand," Kellar persisted, realizing that there was some danger in doing so but more than a little fascinated by what the woman had been telling him. "Frau Heydrich, can you possibly—?"

But Lina Heydrich obviously did not wish to continue, ending the conversation with a strange and rather giddy chuckle an instant before she broke the connection.

Though Felix Kellar had been accustomed to infamies of a varied and deplorable sort during his decade of serving the Nazi regime, he shivered suddenly as he slowly hung up the phone receiver, a deep, unholy chill attaching itself to every inch of his small, thin, fragile-looking frame.

7

My country house!" Erwin Rommel exclaimed as the Mercedes passed through the main gate and up the winding driveway to a baroque residence of stained-glass windows, heavy stone blocks and a massive hand-carved front door, all of which seemed like leftovers from the days of German royalty. Yet it had been maintained in such condition in its tree-sheltered estate setting that it seemed as though it had been built only a few years earlier. "An extraordinary place, I know, but Hitler insists upon this sort of thing for high-ranking officers. I have little doubt that it is his way of guaranteeing the loyalty of his top military men."

"And yet the military of which you speak is riddled with antipathy toward the Nazi regime, a military filled with generals, admirals, and other officers who hate the Führer who seeks to reward them for their supposed loyalty!" Stephen Bartlett pointed out somewhat brashly under the circumstances.

"Even the principled can be lulled into complacency, I am afraid," the field marshal shot back.

"Are you an example of that?"

"No, I am not, but I see that *you* represent a *perfect* specimen of that American recklessness about which I hear so much!"

Bartlett had to admit that he indeed had pushed matters a bit too far.

"Excuse me, sir," he apologized. "I sometimes fail to show as much restraint as perhaps I should."

"I know your purpose," Rommel added. "You want to test my tolerance for such behavior and by that tolerance, you are assuming that you somehow will be able to read how much I can be trusted."

Bartlett chose not to reply.

"Fortunately you have not misjudged me," Rommel assured him, a slight smile curling up the sides of his mouth.

They got out of the Mercedes and approached the front door.

"Is your family here?" Bartlett asked.

"My family is elsewhere," Rommel said cryptically.

Behind them, the contingent of soldiers had taken another driveway to a building set off to one side.

"The men stay in what used to be servants' quarters," the German explained as he noticed that Bartlett had seen this.

"They are your guard?"

"I must say yes, though the idea of protection is repugnant to me."

"Why is that?"

"We are on German soil. It means that the war effort has deteriorated so badly that nowhere are even the officers of my rank safe."

"Or the Führer himself?" Bartlett remarked.

"Some would say that, yes," Rommel said curtly.

A maid opened the door and the two of them walked inside.

"You *are* my prisoner," Rommel said as he saw the American's expression. "This is not a mere charade, you know."

"I have no doubt about that," Bartlett responded immediately without quite the note of conviction that he had intended.

They entered a large, high-ceilinged room in which every wall was lined end-to-end with bookshelves.

"The furniture is beautiful," Bartlett observed as he saw the heavy, handmade pieces from another era.

"Craftsmanship," Rommel told him. "Here and on the battlefield, it is terribly important. It implies tradition, and tradition is an indispensable part of the foundation of any civilization. Without it, there is anarchy."

"The Führer would say that tradition is fine but too much of tradition carries with it the influences of Jews."

"True. But I have found that there is nothing of itself reprehensible about the Jewish character."

"That sounds—"

"Treasonous?" Rommel interrupted. "I suppose, in the present environment, that that might be. But then—"

"The present environment and the actions of the Nazis could be considered in themselves quite treasonous, is that not so?" broke in Bartlett this time.

The field marshal stared at the American then, his blue eyes seemingly analyzing every inch of the man.

"You do indeed risk a great deal speaking as you do," Rommel commented knowingly. "But, then, you cannot be unaware of that danger, so I must assume you know what you are doing."

"The greater risk is yours," Bartlett reminded him.

Rommel nodded.

"So it is," he agreed, sighing, some deep sorrow evident in the weary tone of his voice. "I risk losing my life, as my country has lost its soul."

The German indicated a heavy, dark wooden chair.

"Please sit down," he said, settling into a similar chair opposite Bartlett.

"So many books," Bartlett commented. "Yours?"

"No, they are not, I am sorry to tell you. The previous owner of this estate accumulated the entire collection."

"The house and the grounds were appropriated by the government then?"

"They were."

"Why?"

"The owner happened to be a Jewish financier. He was accused of profiting from Germany's miseries during the 1920s and the early 1930s. Of all the effective symbols appropriated by the Nazis, such a man was the most useful."

Rommel indicated the hundreds of titles with a wave of his right arm.

"I think there is no more telling indication of a man's inner being than the choices he makes for books in his personal library."

"And what did you find here?" Bartlett asked.

"If Jews are, as we have been told over and over, such thoroughly loathsome creatures, if they are mere vermin prowling the dark alleys of any civilized nation, then why do I see the complete works of Shakespeare, biographies of Mozart, Bach, Wagner? There are Bibles, Old and New Testaments, in a variety of languages."

"Are the Bibles here as mere historical items? Or do they perhaps suggest the spirituality of the man?"

"I cannot say for certain," acknowledged Rommel.

He leaned forward.

"In recent weeks, I have taken to reading a particular, rather well-worn edition that I found here," he spoke with great seriousness, "It was published in the German language. As I go through it, I am discovering, very much to my amazement in view of my earlier agnostic skepticism, that certain passages are quite profoundly affecting."

"Which ones?" the American pressed.

Sighing, Rommel fell back against the chair. For a moment he chose not to reply, but to sit quietly, his manner contemplative.

Bartlett saw, in that moment, somebody of exceptionally noble character and human decency, honorably trying to grapple with the demonization of all that he had come to cherish over the fifty-odd years of his life. He saw Rommel as a basically simple man, yet one capable of the grandest military strategy, who was suddenly very weary of a battle of quite another sort going on far behind his country's front lines.

"I read in Romans about God giving an entire group of people over to an evil and corrupt way of life."

Rommel visibly shuddered as he recalled the first chapter of Romans.

"That was written two thousand years ago but it describes the German people at this very moment, and I wonder, how can that be?" he asked, deeply puzzled.

Rommel stood suddenly.

"I know you not at all and yet I am talking like this," he said, angry with himself as he started to pace the tongue-and-groove floor.

"It could be the Holy Spirit prompting you," Bartlett offered.

"In the land of Luther, such a thought is hardly unknown."

"It is more than a thought, sir. It is a fact of life for anyone who truly believes, who opens his soul to—"

"You say *soul?*" Rommel interrupted again. "I see no evidence of souls on the battlefield, only crushed and bloody bodies. I see no hint of souls or humanity or anything of the sort in the men at the helm of the government of this land, only maniacs bent on dragging down everyone else with them. I see—"

He raised a clenched fist in front of him.

"—only Satan reigning supreme," he said, spitting out the words. "May God Himself forgive me for thoughts such as these."

Bartlett stood and walked over to him.

"But, as you must know, it has seldom been otherwise throughout all of history," he pointed out. "What makes a difference is where individuals stand, men such as you and me, the families we raise, the—"

Rommel had had his back to the American. Now he spun around, suddenly facing Stephen Bartlett.

"I *have* come to believe," the field marshal said, the faintest hint of tears in his eyes. "But I am terribly afraid that this faith, this newfound faith that has washed me clean of nihilism and so much else that encumbered my very spirit, that it will somehow render me soft, weak perhaps, unable to go into battle again against the Allies, knowing so very clearly now whom I serve when I do."

He was starting to choke up but fought his way through it.

"How can I ever face any of those demons in Berlin," Rommel continued, "without trying to rip their evil hearts from their bodies before I am killed by the men ordered to protect them?"

"No, no, that can never be the case," Bartlett said, placing a hand on each shoulder. "Faith takes a man, and far from emasculating him, it *prepares* him for what lies ahead. He can go into a den of lions, if necessary, and not fear them, for his body is all that they can touch. . . . His soul is beyond their reach."

"I have not reached an understanding as deep as that," Rommel admitted. "Will you stay with me for a while so we can talk of such matters?"

He noticed an expression of disappointment that had started to flicker across the American's face.

"But then I can imagine how desperately you want to find out about your wife and son," Rommel added. "Let me help you: Since being contacted, I have gone outside of normal channels of communication and have been able to find out that the two of them were just today transferred to Dachau."

"I learned that from Frau Heydrich herself," Bartlett told him. "What can we do to save Natalie and Andrew?"

"Before leaving here to pick you up, I tried to contact Himmler. But I must tell you that communication with Berlin has been temporarily interrupted. Allied bombing raids are responsible, I believe."

"What will you do?" the American asked.

"I will leave in the morning. Berlin can be reached in a few hours if there are no mishaps along the way."

Anticipating Bartlett's insecurity at being left in the care of German troopers, Rommel added, "They are loyal to *me,* you know. For the longest while, I tended to discourage that sort of thing, instilling in my men a far greater loyalty to the nation of Germany. Now I see it is good that a few failed to heed me!"

"And what will you ask of Himmler?"

"I will suggest that it is not worthy of *Deutschland* to take the innocent wife and the innocent son even of a criminal such as Stephen Bartlett and dispose of them in the same manner as with common gutter scum such as Jews and Gypsies."

Rommel could see the open disgust that the American was feeling.

"To communicate with a monster such as Heinrich Himmler, one must speak his language, be aware of his sensibilities, and, above all, appeal to his prejudices," he countered. "Would you rather that I use undefiled words and thoughts and nothing more? Or should I instead say whatever it takes to free your loved ones from a place only Satan and those who follow him so slavishly could approve of?"

Bartlett nodded, though still uncomfortable with the rock-steady reasoning that the German was offering.

"We will have dinner now, you and I, and, I trust, talk some more," Rommel said. Then, thinking of his own wife and their children, he patted the back of the other man, so much taller and broader than he. "Whatever opinion you might have of my approach, please believe me when I say that I shall do everything in my power to see that your loved ones will not perish. If nothing else, Stephen Bartlett, surely you must remember this: If God be for us, who can be against us, my friend?"

Bartlett was not able to go to bed until past midnight. He and Rommel had spent the hours during and since dinner in a discussion that neither would have thought possible just days before.

Lord, I hope that You will guide this good man, Bartlett prayed before falling asleep. *He needs Your protection now even more than on the battlefield.*

He caught his breath as he thought of Natalie and Andrew.

If Rommel can help, please, Lord, prepare the way for him, he added, his body trembling as he wondered what was happening to them at that very moment.

A short time later, as sleep was beginning to come, he heard the sound. It was familiar, a sound his ears had been trained to detect . . . that of a bomb's mechanical timer being set, this one apparently rather makeshift since it seemed louder than it should have been.

Bartlett sat up straight.

Outside.

Another sound.

Footsteps.

How much time have they allowed? he thought, an edge of panic starting in his gut. *How much—?*

Bartlett stood, hurried over to the window in his room, and saw three men running from the house.

Suddenly the door to the bedroom was thrown open.

Field Marshal Rommel stood in the doorway.

"You heard them too!" he exclaimed, his expression tense.

"Yes . . . a bomb. Perhaps more than one. I saw three men going for cover."

"More," Rommel corrected. "Already among the trees."

"Because of me," Bartlett lamented as he threw on his clothes, regretting that he had gotten such a man implicated.

"You are probably correct," Rommel admitted. "Here, take this."

In the German's left hand was a Luger.

"If the attackers are all around us," the American asked, "then where can we go?"

"You and my men will go into a tunnel directly underneath this house. I shall remain here."

"You cannot do that," insisted Bartlett. "They will execute you on the spot or else take you back to Berlin as a prisoner."

"I think not, Stephen."

"But—" the American started to protest.

"You see, it so happens that I know one of them, the leader," Rommel explained, "I caught a glimpse of his face for an instant. He is a foul man, to be sure, but one who has publicly expressed some admiration for me since the war began. I cannot believe that he is entirely committed to this attack."

"If you think you can stop whoever it is by mere conversation, why do you send the rest of us away?"

Rommel hesitated then, not accustomed to being questioned in that manner by a stranger, especially an American.

"I am afraid that quite soon I shall be coming to the end of any usefulness I might have had for *Deutschland* or any other cause, for that matter," he responded. "The war is being lost on all fronts. My leaders are not worthy of my allegiance. I can see only pain, only the greatest suffering ahead.

"But, for you, Stephen, there is much more. You have a mission, saving your loved ones, and after that, the Allies unquestionably will need you for other missions in the final days before Germany is defeated. You serve God. You deserve victory. As for me, the devil has been my master far too long."

"I still cannot—," Bartlett protested.

"You have no choice!" Rommel reminded him. "Do not forget that you are, after all, still my prisoner."

Three troopers came up behind the field marshal.

"To the tunnel," Rommel ordered, turning toward his men. "Treat the American as one of us."

He looked back at Bartlett.

"I think I shall survive somehow," he said. "I think I shall survive not so much for myself, perhaps, but because God intends for me to help those you love, Stephen Bartlett."

The first bomb went off a few seconds later.

8

While not comfortable with this latest mission, Felix Kellar was committed to being nothing less than a patriotic professional. He had been serving the Führer proficiently since the mid- to late 1930s, including his part in the infamous *Kristallnacht*, which the Allies called "The Night of the Broken Glass."

This watershed fifteen-hour period of maniacal rampage was precipitated when a bitter Polish Jew named Herschel Grynszpan assassinated Ernst vom Rath, third secretary of the German Embassy in Paris, thus providing the Nazis the excuse they had been seeking to begin an all-out campaign of intimidation against what they called the Jewish vermin who had been plaguing the *Deutschland* for far too many years.

Heydrich asked me to participate in the retaliation that would be unleashed against those repugnant people, Kellar remembered. *I agreed to do so, and with appreciation. I was becoming bored, with so little else to do.*

Virtually all places of Jewish worship throughout Germany as well as Austria were destroyed during *Kristallnacht*, as ordered by the man who in a few years would come to be called the Butcher of Prague. During the course of those fifteen terrifying hours, more than a hundred synagogues were systematically burned to the ground by uniformed soldiers, and nearly eighty others were demolished, many with frightened Jews trapped inside.

In addition, frenzied bands of zealous, out-of-control Nazi sympathizers roamed the cities and countryside farms, screaming out their hatred in venomous and often blasphemous epithets. Law-enforcement officials offered no resistance when these fanatic hordes razed more than seventy-five hundred Jewish-owned stores, many of which had been in business for generations.

Ah, what Goebbels said afterward, Kellar remembered with admiration, though without the enthusiasm he had felt at the time. *What a forthright man!*

"We shall discipline the Jews in other ways, you know," Goebbels had told Goering, Kellar, and others three days later. "They will no longer be allowed to use our various public parks and toilet facilities. We shall send their kind running into the forests where they can live among the other beasts. Who can disagree that they should be especially at home with the elk, which also possess hooked noses?"

There was great laughter at that remark, Kellar's the heartiest of all.

But events subsequent to *Kristallnacht* proved to be even more brutal than a veteran such as himself had envisioned.

It was one thing to exile them to the wilderness. It was quite another to build camps, gas them to death, and incinerate their bodies, and . . .

Kellar shuddered as he recalled what, just months earlier, he had witnessed of the Mengele experiments at Auschwitz.

But still I have continued to cooperate. Still I have never failed to obey whatever the orders are given to me by my superiors. I have not ceased rounding up groups of Jews and Gypsies and sending them away. Whatever happened after they were out of my hands was not my responsibility.

Yet now Kellar was in service not directly to the Führer but to a deranged woman who was sworn to a personal campaign of vengeance, whatever the cost to her and those who were allied with her in it.

Sometimes having good sources who are loyal to me and able to track down whomever I please can be a curse, especially since I have acquired some fame over the years because of this, he told himself. *Look at how it has gotten me into this—*

"Sir, sir," a voice penetrated his reverie.

Kellar glanced up. He had been leaning against the trunk of a large tree several hundred feet from the back entrance to the house where, from his sources, he had guessed Rommel and the American would head.

"The bombs have been planted," a young aide told him. "We had to kill three soldiers, but we used knives; no shots were fired."

"In the tunnel too?" Kellar asked.

"At the very end," the young man pointed out, smiling somewhat crookedly. "If any try to escape that way, as I can only suspect they will, they may well think they have succeeded, only to be blown to bits in the very next instant before they ever make it aboveground."

"The tunnel bombs have been set by tripwires?"

"Yes. The ones around the house are timed. They should go off in less than five minutes, as planned."

"Good, good," Kellar replied, trying to speak in a manner that suggested genuine appreciation, an appreciation he did not feel.

"Field Marshal Rommel deserves death," the aide added. "He has dishonored this nation by his actions."

Kellar spun around on one heel.

"What about the man's victories on the battlefields of Africa?" he demanded. "Are those to be forgotten in the midst of the rubble we shall be creating?"

The aide was startled into silence by the ferocity of the other's response.

"He makes one mistake," Kellar added, "and we are now so eager to crucify someone with such genius!"

"Sir," the young man ventured more than a bit nervously, "you should not be angry at me. You are the one who accepted this assignment. The other men and I are simply obeying orders that you have given us."

Kellar nodded, his anger spent.

"What you say is true," he confessed. "I—"

The first bomb exploded a split second later.

"The others are set to go off at thirty-second intervals," the aide remarked. "By the time we go against the house, it will be little more than a blackened and empty shell. There is every reason to doubt that anyone inside will be left in a position to resist. As you know, however, we are prepared for that eventuality."

He hesitated, swallowing quickly several times, his demeanor changing, becoming less confident; more of the insecurity of his youth was coming to the surface.

"What is it?" Kellar asked, alarmed at what he was seeing in a normally well-composed aide. "Are you ill?"

"The artwork, the books that are in the house," the other man said, his tone forlorn, "such a massive collection compiled by that Jew financier. Few of them will be saved, I am sure, Sir. I must say that that does seem a pity. After all, the whole lot of them was bought with money extorted from the people of Germany since the end of World War I. How sad that such items also must be sacrificed."

At the thought of that tragic waste of part of a nation's heritage, the normally callous and sometimes oafish Felix Kellar looked away so that the other man would not see the emotions playing across his face.

"Who does the greater evil?" he murmured.

"I do not understand your meaning, sir," the aide acknowledged, frowning in puzzlement.

"It is obvious that there were some matters that your days as a Hitler Youth never taught you," Kellar said cryptically.

"I wonder how that can be, sir? Were we not supposed to be given the mind of the Führer himself?"

Kellar smiled, an expression of profound irony on his face.

"That should be a comfort to all of us," he whispered sarcastically, "a comfort, to be sure."

Obeying the orders of Field Marshal Rommel, five SS troopers followed Stephen Bartlett into the tunnel, the entrance of which was located in the basement of that mansion-like house, just a few yards away from the area designated as a wine cellar. It had been dug some thirty years earlier, according to what Rommel had told them minutes before, an intended escape route for members of the Kaiser's family.

"Germany was bled dry after the war," a tall, almost bony-framed trooper named Gustav Dobrik remarked. "Money-obsessed Jews grabbed this estate quickly enough when it was selling for a cheap price. Now *we* are the ones who have taken to running from our own kind. What kind of sense does that make?"

"No, you are quite wrong," another, much broader-looking trooper, Hans Hauswirth, countered. "The ones who have begun attacking that house are not *our* kind at all. They are probably Nazis. And the Nazis will never be *our* kind, Gustav. Their tactics play right into the hands of the Allies."

"How can you justify saying that?" Dobrik demanded. "How can you embarrass yourself like that?"

"It is truth, Gustav, and truth is all we ever have that means anything. The Nazis feed the international Jew propaganda machine. If we were to stop slaughtering the Jews, we would have a moral right supporting us that now has been lost to our cause. No one listens to cries of morality and decency on the one hand while mass murder is being committed by the protesters on the other!"

"But our *cause* is precisely that—the total elimination of any and all Jew scum from German soil," Dobrik shot back with great passion. "Take that away, I ask, and what do we have left?"

"I agree to a certain extent, my friend. Of course I do, or I would not be fighting alongside you. But it must be done without an entire nation becoming captive to barbarism in the process. Do we not descend to their despicable level when we murder helpless Jewish men, women, and children by the hundreds of thousands?

"I say this: All of us become *worse* than the Jews ever could have been when we take a single life in such a manner, let alone the great numbers we all have heard about. Instead we should merely deport them to the West where England and the United States will have the responsibility for the swine.

"Soon enough, we all know, the Allies will come to regret giving any of the Jews protective asylum in the first place. Their kind are perfectly capable of wearing out their own welcome without taking us down into the gutter along with them. Don't you see how true this is? Answer me: Don't you?"

Dobrik fell silent as they continued walking through the foul-smelling tunnel, obviously realizing that his comrade had made a point worth considering.

For his part, Stephen Bartlett saw what a curious position he was in. He could hardly agree with the philosophy of either man, but he needed them both and the three other troopers with them—if he was to have any chance of making it to Dachau and freeing Natalie and Andrew.

Hauswirth is anti-Semitic but favors a gentler approach to solving the so-called Jewish question, he started to tell himself. *Yet his attitude is still based upon . . .*

Before the group had entered the tunnel, one of the troopers had offered to walk on ahead of the others.

"Look out for snakes," two of them joked.

"Pray that they aren't *Jewish* snakes; they're the worst of all, you know," added the third. "Their fangs look like Jew noses!"

Grimacing, Bartlett recoiled from such talk but decided he was not in any position to speak out against it.

If I say anything provocative, they might rebel against the orders Rommel gave them, he told himself. *They could reasonably claim that part of the tunnel collapsed on me and I was killed in a matter of seconds.*

He stopped himself.

Oh, God! he exclaimed. *How easily—!*

The sound of an explosion ahead wrenched him from that thought.

"A bomb!" Dobrik shouted. "This place may be filled with them. We've just been lucky so far."

Bartlett spoke up, "Let me see what's happened. I'll go on ahead. Lend me a flashlight, will you?"

Dobrik held out the one he had been using.

"Field Marshal Rommel told us that you know a great deal about munitions, explosives, that sort of thing," he said, trying to supress a note of admiration in his voice but not entirely succeeding. "He said you may be the world's leading expert, in fact. That is why the Allies consider you to be so important."

"I guess what you say is true," Bartlett replied modestly.

"How could a man like you be stupid enough to waste time on vermin?" Dobrik asked coldly.

Bartlett could no longer hold back.

"To the Jews, it is the Germans who fit that description," he observed. "To the French as well. The Dutch despise the Nazis. Many of the Scandinavians certainly do. Shall I go on? Or have you gotten the point?"

Dobrik's anger and disgust registered on his face.

Bartlett paused, then added, "Gustav, tell me: Have you ever been inside a concentration camp run by the Nazis?"

"It matters not!" Dobrik retorted as he shook his head. "You cannot accuse anyone here. None of us are Nazis!"

"Those who serve the devil are destined to become as devils themselves."

Dobrik reached out a hand that had been clenched into a fist.

"Go," he said, "do what you can, Stephen Bartlett. Afterward, you and I will have to settle this."

"As you wish," Bartlett replied, nodding.

The American turned and, holding the flashlight firmly, walked ahead as cautiously as he could.

Behind him, he heard Dobrik utter a profanity.

A minute or two later, Bartlett came upon what was left of the body of the trooper, buried amidst the rubble.

There could be more bombs than the one that caused this, he reasoned. *As bad as all this looks, I don't think this bomb was all that powerful.*

He pointed the beam of light at the tunnel wall ahead of him, aiming it left, then right, then at the ceiling.

Telltale wires . . . tripwires.

Those guys were apparently in a hurry, he assumed. *They didn't have time to be as careful as they should have been.*

Someone less experienced might have decided simply to cut the wires, but Bartlett knew that the slightest motion could detonate one bomb after the other.

It wasn't accidental or careless after all! Those responsible were counting on the ignorance of anyone who spotted the wires. Even if nobody noticed, there was still every chance that, in the darkness, the wires would be stepped on anyway. Either way, they would get what they were after . . . our deaths!

Farther on, he could glimpse other wires.

A gauntlet.

Again and again, a bomb would have to be uncovered and disabled until no more were left. But he had no idea how many he needed to deal with in a short, tense time. He risked missing just the one that would kill him, and further collapse the tunnel, dooming the men behind him.

Five minutes passed.

He found three others, unhooked the relatively simple and obviously makeshift firing mechanisms, and threw each to one side.

As Bartlett reached out for a fourth, then stumbled back, he noticed something black an inch or so away, *something that moved!*

The bomb had been placed in a section containing a large nest of viper-like black-bodied snakes, their skin smooth and faintly shiny, some as big as four feet long and several inches thick. The shaking of the tunnel caused by the earlier explosion had split open the hollowed-out nest where they had settled. Now dozens of them were emerging like large, slimy worms.

9

Hans Hauswirth heard the American scream.

"Let him go," Gustav Dobrik said. "He deserves nothing from us."

Hauswirth spun around on one heel.

"He deserves everything," he countered. "He is a link with sanity. And *this* is not the time to debate what happens to the man."

Ahead of them they could hear the sounds of frantic movement.

"He is the *enemy!*" Dobrik blurted.

"As well as the Jew?" Hauswirth said, shouting louder than the other man. "Why did you not add that? I would agree with you there, my friend. The Jew indeed is our enemy. But *this* American is not."

"It is impossible to separate the two, Gustav. The American represents a massive effort to *save* the Jews. Why is it that you fail to see this?"

"I hate them as well," Hauswirth went on. "I just do not think that murdering them or letting the American die is the answer. And you *know* that Rommel agrees. I also realize how much you admire the man."

Dobrik nodded reluctantly.

"I will join you," he said.

The other troopers volunteered but were told to stay where they were.

Hauswirth and Dobrik walked slowly ahead, neither of them having a hint of what to expect. They found the American pressed against the eastern wall of the tunnel. All around him were coal-black snakes.

"One was beginning to crawl up my leg!" Stephen Bartlett called out when he noticed the two troopers. "I had to get them off. I had to—"

Perspiration covered Dobrik's face.

"I hate them!" he exclaimed, panic momentarily grabbing him. "Even the American cannot die in this manner."

Both men raised their guns and started to aim.

"*No!*" Bartlett yelled. "There are tripwires all over this area. If you aren't careful, you could bring down tons of rock and soil on us."

Dobrik was frustrated.

"Then Hauswirth and I turn and go back, leaving you here— is that what you are saying?" he spoke irritably.

"You'll have to get closer," Bartlett said. "You'll have to aim at them one by one. I know where at least some of the tripwires are. If a snake's too close, I can tell you."

"What if it is?" Dobrik asked. "What will we do then?"

"Distract it. Get it away by throwing rocks at it. Then you can shoot!"

Dobrik's gun hand was shaking.

"It will be all right, Gustav," Hauswirth told him. "Just pretend it's a Jew each time. You might even have fun at it!"

Dobrik shot him a glance that shut up Hauswirth in an instant.

"That's *exactly* what I'll do," he retorted.

He bent down, just a couple of feet away from one of the snakes that glistened ominously in the beam of his flashlight.

"What if it strikes at me?" he asked.

"Duck," Hauswirth replied.

Dobrik held his breath, aiming the Luger with his other hand, his finger resting lightly on the trigger, then tightening just seconds before he fired.

"Bull's-eye!" he exclaimed proudly.

"Gustav!" Hauswirth yelled. "To your left!"

Dobrik jerked his head in that direction.

From the ceiling of the tunnel—another one! Apparently the snakes nested all over that area.

Dobrik aimed and fired again, striking this second target with equal accuracy.

The snakes were being drawn toward the two other men and away from Bartlett.

"Another pistol," the American called. "Throw it to me."

"Only these two," Hauswirth started to say.

Footsteps behind him.

"Take this one!" another of the troopers called to him.

The pistol fell an inch or two short of Bartlett's outreached hands, right into the path of a sinewy black shape.

He bent down, hoping the creature would crawl past, ignoring the cold metal weapon. He forgot that snakes were drawn by heat and his body, dripping perspiration, was sending out wave after wave of it.

The snake paused, immobile, looking for the moment like a strand of inanimate black rope.

Bartlett started to reach for the Luger. He would have to grab it in an instant and at the same time shoot the snake.

He hesitated, noticing a sliver of wire to its left.

A bomb! he exclaimed to himself. *I told the others to be so careful and now here I am, faced with* . . .

He swallowed, then held his breath, his arm jerking forward, toward the pistol, his fingers closing around it, pulling it back, the snake struck toward him, so close he could feel its wet skin brushing his hand, then falling back, ready to strike again.

Bartlett fired, missed, then hit the snake just above its mouth.

"More of them!" he could hear someone exclaim.

"Don't start firing at will," Bartlett begged. "You'd never be able to imagine how rigged this area is."

"But they're everywhere," protested another voice, particularly shrill, that he recognized as Gustav Dobrik's.

"One by one," Bartlett repeated grimly, "at close range."

Shots were fired. He stopped breathing, steeling himself for an explosion.

What must have been a minute or two passed. Finally the rapid fire was joined by several screams. Bartlett shone his flashlight in that direction. He saw several men covered with snakes as they fell to their knees.

Dobrik stumbled toward him.

"Hans, hurry!" he was muttering, half-looking over his shoulder.

Hauswirth was caught in the illumination from the American's flashlight, his hands flailing wildly in front of him, his head looking like a grotesque, bloody, venom-splattered Medusa.

Dobrik swung around, dropping his own flashlight in the process, and saw Hauswirth just as the body fell less than two feet from him. The snakes immediately let go and crawled in his direction.

"Stephen, help me, please!" he screamed. "Where do I go? Where—?"

"Straight ahead," Bartlett told him, uncomfortable with the task of saving a man who favored the extermination of Jews, even though he was not a Nazi. "Listen to me. Listen to every word, Gustav."

The American told him where to place each foot.

"Slowly," he admonished the other man. "Be very steady. You are right between two tripwires now. You don't have a quarter of an inch to spare."

Obviously terrified, Dobrik followed the path Bartlett had indicated, the American's flashlight providing the only illumination.

"Don't look back," Bartlett told him. "You might lose your balance. You have to remain completely steady as you go."

"But what about the snakes?" Dobrik said, his voice not much below a scream. "Can you see where they are?"

"Inches away, Gustav."

"Shoot them!"

"Not close enough. I might hit one of the wires."

"But how do I know that you—?"

"Shut up, Gustav," Bartlett interrupted. "If you die, so do I, remember that. Your body will probably fall right across a wire. I'll be blown up with you."

Seconds passed.

Dobrik had nearly reached the American.

"Stop!" Bartlett said harshly, chilling the other man's blood.

"What is it?" the German asked, trying to hide how he felt, trying to ignore the panic that was squeezing his insides.

"Another wire, Gustav, this one directly across your path."

"What do I do?"

"Step over it, but very slowly," Bartlett replied. "You cannot touch it by more than a hair or it will detonate a bomb, wherever it happens to be placed."

"How . . . how do I know if I've cleared it, Stephen? How can I—?"

"Look straight down. I'll shine my light in that direction."

Dobrik could barely see the treacherous thin wire that stretched from one side of the tunnel to the other.

"My boot is just *under* it!" Dobrik exclaimed, nausea starting to overwhelm his stomach.

"Then step back slowly."

"I cannot. These boots have seen much service. They are scratched, the leather uneven. One tiny flap of leather on my right boot is caught on the wire!"

Bartlett paused, thinking of what to do. There were just two choices: One, he could try to lift the wire just enough for Dobrik to pull back his boot, but this risked triggering the bomb if there was too much stress on the wire; two, Dobrik could try to slide out of the boot and leave it there with the wire.

"Gustav, this is what we'll do," Bartlett finally instructed the German. "I'm going to go to my knees and hold the boot. You've got to get your foot out of it with the least possible movement or we're both doomed."

"It fits tightly," Dobrik acknowledged. "I am not sure that I can . . ."

"If you find that it's impossible," Bartlett interrupted, "the only other course of action is to cut the boot open from below the knee to just above the heel, giving you a little more room to move."

"Do that! Yes, that is what you must do!"

"I have no knife."

"I do. It is in my back pocket. I shall try to get it now."

He groped behind him, temporarily throwing himself somewhat off balance. The wire moved slightly.

"Careful, Gustav!" Bartlett cautioned.

Dobrik steadied himself.

"I have the knife now," he said tensely. "Take it."

Bartlett walked very slowly forward, reached out, grabbed the pocketknife, and opened it. Then he got down on his knees, holding the flashlight with his left hand and cutting into the side of the boot with the knife in his right.

"Stephen!" Dobrik said suddenly. "Above you! A snake. It has come through a crack in the ceiling."

Almost immediately, Bartlett felt it drop onto his back.

"Stephen, it's—!" the other man gasped.

"I know . . ."

Bartlett felt it crawling toward his head, felt its cold skin soon touch the back of his neck, felt its tongue dart out, tasting his earlobe.

Time was running out.

Bartlett reached around the side of his head, praying that he could grip the snake at just the right spot, directly behind its eyes and jaw.

Now!

The creature was strong, flailing in his grasp.

Bartlett sliced it with the pocketknife, digging into the top of its head and ripping into its small brain, then twisting the weapon in a complete circle, the body now limp. He tossed it to one side.

He was shaking.

Dobrik looked at him with some sympathy.

"You are brave," he said simply.

"I wonder where the bravery is when there is no choice involved, Gustav," the American murmured.

He returned to slicing open Dobrik's boot.

"Can you lift up now?" he asked.

The German grimaced as he started pulling his leg up.

"I think it will be okay," he said. "I think . . ."

He seemed to be struggling.

"No . . . I cannot seem to . . . to pull it all the way out."

"I'll cut down just a bit more," Bartlett told him.

As he was approaching the ankle, his hand slipped, and the knife sliced into Dobrik's heel, blood seeping up through the gash, down the side of the boot, and onto the dirt floor of the tunnel.

The other man let out a sudden cry and started to fall forward.

Bartlett reached up and caught him.

"Please forgive me!" Bartlett begged. "God knows I tried not to—."

"Go ahead, Stephen," Dobrik interrupted, though it was obvious that he spoke with great difficulty. "Finish what you were doing. Neither of us has any real hope of survival if you fail in this."

"But *can* you remain standing, Gustav?" Bartlett asked, deeply concerned. "You're bleeding badly. And the pain must be—"

"I have fought worse pain than this," Dobrik interrupted. "Trust me to warn you if I am unable to hold out."

Feeling more than a touch of admiration, Bartlett proceeded to pull the knife out of his heel in one quick, steady move, hoping any damage would be minimized.

Dobrik gasped and wavered, then steadied himself.

As he noticed the expression on the American's face, he spoke up, his voice strained and hoarse, "Stephen, do not feel . . . guilty. I know it was only an accident . . . I am not . . . a loathsome devil . . . all the time, you know."

Surprised, Bartlett nodded appreciatively, and then continued slicing through the remaining two inches of tough old leather.

Field Marshal Erwin Rommel was sitting at a large round table in the midst of the room filled with a thousand books when Felix

Kellar and his men burst through the door. Their guns were raised, and they were obviously prepared to shoot.

Rommel looked up rather casually and said, "Thank you for preserving the most important room in this monument to Jewish excess."

He saw their startled expressions.

"There are a sufficient number of chairs to accommodate you," he added, "and quite enough books to command your undivided attention."

Kellar lowered his pistol, as did the others.

"I have heard a great deal about you," he admitted.

"How much of that has come from Lina Heydrich?"

Kellar sat down across the table from Rommel, his men taking chairs on either side of him.

"You are staring at me," Rommel observed after a minute or two.

"I am," Kellar replied.

"Because you are wondering how someone such as myself could ever serve a corrupt Nazi regime."

The other man caught his breath.

"You have no response?" Rommel went on. "The answer is not a complex one. I serve Germany, not the Nazis."

"When have they stopped being one and the same, Field Marshal Rommel?" Kellar countered.

"When Jews were herded into the camps and exterminated."

"But you loathe their kind as much as I, as do others."

"I loathe what they did to this country. But I also contend that we cannot rise successfully from the ashes of the past if we act far, far worse than those who try to bury us in those ashes in the first place!"

Rommel's eyes narrowed.

"But then why I am speaking in this manner to you, someone who serves a woman whose passion for vengeance—"

"Stop!" Kellar demanded as he slammed his fist down on the table.

"Stop from what? Telling the truth? You gather together your little band of hired assassins and send them against me. Shall I call that the noble act of—?"

Kellar shot to his feet.

"You shall die right now!" he bellowed.

"If that is your wish," Rommel said, "I can hardly stop you. But let it be, this final moment of my life, as I am opening this Bible in front of me and reading about the acts of men emboldened by a far greater Master than any you and I have *ever* served."

Kellar had raised his Luger and aimed it straight at Rommel's forehead, his finger tightened around the trigger.

Beside the Bible was a sheet of paper. On it was a cable message.

"Reinhard Heydrich had nothing to do with saving your son," Rommel spoke slowly. "I must say that I was the one who stepped in."

For a moment, Kellar continued holding the gun steady, perspiration forming on his forehead as he tried to deal with that information without showing any emotional reaction.

Finally he lowered the Luger and sat down, as did the men on either side of him.

"How did you know anything about me?" Kellar asked, surprised. "I should be a stranger to you."

"For a moment, I saw your face among the trees," Rommel responded. "I recognized you immediately."

"Because of André?"

Rommel nodded, smiling.

Kellar's shoulders sank.

My husband saved the life of your son. . . . You said, in return, that he could have your soul if he wanted it.

"Frau Heydrich told me that monstrous husband of hers was responsible," Kellar told him. "She used that story to get me to do what I have been here to do."

"André was with me at the front lines in Africa," Rommel explained patiently. "I found your son to be one of my finest young men. After he was wounded, I had him shipped back to Berlin so he would receive expert medical care, which wouldn't have been possible under battleground conditions. I knew that I couldn't let such a brave, fine human being die so soon."

"But what happened?" Kellar asked. "He was dying. Someone called in Hitler's personal physician. I never knew who was behind it until that woman told me that her husband arranged everything. My son was in no condition to know what was going on and tell me the right of it."

"That must have seemed wildly out of character for the man named the Butcher of Prague, surely you realized that."

"I suppose it would have if I had thought about it. But I assumed she told me the truth since it was hardly an incident that was to become common knowledge. As far as I was concerned, it seemed a miracle that Andrés life was saved. For anyone else, it would have been just a statistic involving yet another young man wounded in battle. I assumed she could not have known if Reinhard Heydrich had not been involved."

Kellar's eyes narrowed, and his expression turned suspicious. "How *did* she find out?"

"You have quite a reputation for service," Rommel offered. "Is it so strange that Lina Heydrich got a file on you and searched it for clues to how—?"

"—she could have my soul on a silver platter," Kellar finished the sentence for him. "She saw your name in the file, not her husband's."

"Think of the irony, Felix. She eliminates me and gets the American at the same time. And you would never have known."

"What can I do now?" the other man asked, his voice trembling.

"You can get me to Berlin."

"To stop whatever is happening to this American's loved ones?"

"Yes! She told you?"

"She hinted something."

"Felix, you must catch up with Stephen Bartlett, then accompany him and my men on to Dachau."

"I *will* do that!" Kellar declared, breathing faster, and with obvious relief.

"I shall give you a letter," Rommel said. "It will explain matters. I do not want the American mistaking you for an adversary."

10

Gustav Dobrik's foot was throbbing.

He and the American had come more than a mile from the tunnel exit. The exertion had weakened him. Ordinarily he could run such a distance and not be affected. But the pain was severe, and he had to stop.

"You are quite strong," Dobrik said as he settled back against a tree trunk. "I could sense that even someone as heavy as I leaning against you seemed to you more like a toy than a full-grown man."

Bartlett smiled.

"The propaganda films I've seen during the past few years emphasize the physical conditioning of German men," he said as he sat next to the German. "I am sure you would have done well if the situation had been reversed."

"If that were true, I might not have carried you at all," Dobrik admitted with apparent discomfort.

Bartlett appreciated the other man's candor.

"We cannot go back," he observed. "How well do you know this territory, Gustav? I, for one, know virtually nothing about it. There wasn't time for a security briefing by my superiors, I'm afraid."

"Very little. This was a special assignment with Rommel. The other men and I were chosen by the Führer himself."

"Were your own views about Jews part of it?"

"The Führer knows those upon whom he can depend."

The two men were sitting in a clearing among the tall, old trees. To their left was a towering peak in that stretch of the mountain range. To their right was a winding dirt road. Straight ahead, the ground sloped down rather gradually to the sparsely populated valley which, at that point, was not far below them.

"So pretty this time of year," Bartlett remarked, wistfully appreciating the beauty of that region.

"But wait until the winter roars in," Dobrik told him. "Any battles that have to be fought here at that time of year would make some others seem like the stuff of a child's playtime."

"Any partisan activity?"

"There is partisan activity *everywhere.*"

Bartlett's eyes widened.

"So *that's* why you were assigned to Rommel."

"To protect him, of course."

"No, I think it's more than that."

Dobrik turned sharply, grimacing from a sudden burst of pain.

"What can you be suggesting?" he asked. "I have no idea what you mean."

"The Field Marshal's support of the regime in Berlin has been softening for some time," Bartlett pointed out. "I doubt that that's common knowledge but I have to believe that it causes concern among Himmler and his crowd."

"Are you trying to tell me that the Desert Fox himself could become a traitor, given the right circumstances?"

The American did not answer directly but added, instead, "If this area has more than negligible activity by patriots fed up with Nazi atrocities, it would be an ideal spot to send Rommel on the pretext of giving him a time of rest and recuperation. The man cannot be plugged into everything. He would hardly know about this."

"You have been here only a short while. How is it that you have arrived at this sort of conclusion?"

"That home, now undoubtedly destroyed, was financed by considerable Jewish wealth. The books inside are worth a fortune, again bought by Jewish money. As Rommel and I arrived, I noticed an old sign, half-hidden by leaves, that hadn't been destroyed yet—on it was a tarnished but still visible Star of David. A bit farther back, there were the remains of what seemed to be a small synagogue."

Dobrik swallowed hard several times.

"A colony of Jews once lived in this area, is that what you are telling me?" he asked a bit stupidly.

"It is. They either were captured and sent to one of the camps or some of them managed to flee into the surrounding forest and mountains."

"Where they remain as partisans, awaiting the day when they can return!"

Bartlett applauded that statement.

"If we can make contact with a partisan cadre, I suspect we can get the help we need," he pointed out.

Dobrik was showing his years of anti-Semitism.

"I think I would rather die!" he declared contemptuously.

"Than accept *Jewish* help?"

"Yes, yes, *yes!*"

"How can you say that?" Bartlett probed. "You are intelligent, well-educated, yet you have fallen for—"

"You overheard what Hauswirth and I were discussing," Dobrik interrupted. "Need I repeat myself?"

Suddenly, Bartlett's head shot up straight.

"Time out!" he blurted. "Listen!"

Dobrik fell silent instantly, cocking his own head back toward the sound of voices.

"They have to be looking for you and me, Stephen, but thinking that the rest are also here," he whispered. "Who can be responsible for this whole ridiculous exercise? The group of us were assigned to the greatest military leader this nation has! Who could *ever* attempt anything like an assault against the Desert Fox?"

"I have no doubt about the answer, Gustav," Bartlett replied. "I can only suppose it is Lina Heydrich."

He told Dobrik about what had happened days before.

"I would have thought the Jews instead were in on it," the German replied, his eyes narrow in reflexive hatred.

"I hope you will realize someday that pure evil has no racial stamp or exclusivity to it," Bartlett countered.

He helped Dobrik to stand.

They had to get down the slope ahead of them to the valley below. And beyond that, there could be no additional stops for rest until both were sure that the men tracking them had not continued the pursuit.

"Can you make it, Gustav?" Bartlett asked.

They were at the edge, looking down, hundreds of feet to the bottom. Sharp-looking rocks jutted out from the mountainside, along with small trees and shrubs. From that distance, numerous patches of dirt seemed no firmer than loose sand.

"What will we hold on to?" Dobrik asked, alarmed. "We have no ropes, no one to support us!"

"You're talking about textbook precision," Bartlett reminded him, "the way everything *should* be. It's all theoretical to a degree."

Dobrik looked embarrassed, all the more so because the American had hit upon a compelling truth.

"Our instructors were so proud," he acknowledged. "They deemed us more than a match for any Allied opposition."

"German soldiers *have* been the toughest adversaries. But, I think, racial pride and worship of the Führer overtook the training process at some point and the whole process unraveled. A mentality of 'we can do no wrong' crept in, and procedures became inexcusably sloppy. But that strong German ego could never admit it, so the sloppiness has continued."

"All right," Dobrik told him, "go ahead. I'll follow your example."

"Don't worry, Gustav. Everyone has fears. Being afraid of heights is no crime, even by Aryan standards."

The German's eyes widened at the insight this stranger had just shown.

"We go down inch by inch," Bartlett replied. "I'll start by digging out hand holes in the dirt as much as I can. The rest of the time, you'll have to do what I do, using rocks or plants or both to grab, hoping they won't pull loose. It's not going to be easy but we can't go back, Gustav. Behind us, well, there's no telling how far the attackers have fanned out. Nor do we have any idea the number of them who are after us right now."

Dobrik nodded, then added cynically, "But how do I know you will not just let me slide to my death?"

"If Rommel trusted you and the others, I don't see how I can justify trying to second-guess a man like that!"

"Perhaps trust is your Achilles heel, Stephen Bartlett."

"Perhaps mistrust is *yours*, Gustav Dobrik."

"Touché!" the German spoke as he nodded with reluctant appreciation. "I have never respected men who would allow me to intimidate them."

A moment later, they started the descent.

Felix Kellar and his men approached as Stephen Bartlett and Gustav Dobrik were halfway down to the valley. He leaned over the edge, shouting to the two of them, but neither could make out what he was saying.

We must stop those two! Kellar thought, with some degree of desperation. *They cannot make it by themselves. The closer they come to*

Dachau, the greater the chance that they will be intercepted by an SS patrol.

"After the American and whoever it is with him!" he ordered. "We must get to them before they escape or are cornered by some passing . . ."

The six men with him waited impatiently for him to finish speaking, then jumped down the mountainside, all of them trained in such feats, working their way along the mountainside much faster than Dobrik and the American were managing. They were eager to help, all greatly moved by what they had been told earlier by such a great war hero. Kellar followed directly behind, touching his chest once with his fingers as he anticipated being able to hand over to them the letter from Field Marshal Rommel.

The widow will not like what is happening this day, he told himself, not without satisfaction. *I can see her fit of rage now!*

Felix Kellar had no way of anticipating what would happen next, and as a result no defense against the bullets that were fired from hidden places by hidden men who would stand beside his battered body in a matter of minutes and chortle over what they had done.

11

Bartlett and Dobrik had just made it to the valley, their pursuers not far behind, when the rifle fire commenced. They hit the ground immediately.

"We were being watched all along, I think," Dobrik whispered.

The men behind them on the mountainside had no time to do anything but scream out in surrender. They could not resist. Several were wounded but able to hold on as they climbed down the rest of the way.

Only Felix Kellar toppled, falling from the slope, his body landing not far from Stephen Bartlett.

Alive.

He was still alive.

He managed to turn toward the American and tried to say something, but the words came out at first as pain-filled gibberish.

Bartlett crawled up to him.

"Pocket . . ." Kellar managed to say coherently, indicating which one he meant. "In . . . my . . . pocket."

Bartlett reached into it and pulled out a sheet of blood-stained paper.

A letter from Rommel.

"You were coming to help us!" Bartlett said after reading what the field marshal had written. "You were—"

"I . . . cannot . . . sanction . . . what . . . that . . . woman . . . was . . . doing . . ."

Trembling, Kellar reached out his left hand toward the American, and Bartlett took it in his own.

"You . . . must . . . tell . . . them . . . my . . . men . . . will . . . help. . . . *Tell them that!*" he added, groaning, as blood dribbled out the corners of his mouth.

Those men, hands held up, emerged from the nearby forest and came to stand next to Kellar in time to hear what he was saying.

All murmured assent.

"This barbarity cannot go on," one said. "Germans killing Germans just because they happen to be Jews—or are friendly to those people!"

Blood continued to dribble out of Kellar's mouth.

"Help me to stand . . . ," he asked Bartlett. "I want to face them . . . I want to tell them how ashamed I am of . . . of—"

Bartlett grabbed his right arm; Dobrik held the left. Together they lifted him up as straight as they could.

A dozen rugged-looking men surrounded them.

"You *are* the Allies' very special agent," spoke one of them after just a few seconds. "Your description was accurate. You *are* a very large man."

He turned to Kellar.

"You are not unknown to us either," he said as he raised the butt of his rifle toward Kellar's temple.

"*No!*" Bartlett said. "He needs help. He doesn't deserve punishment."

He handed the small blood-stained message to the other man, whose eyes widened as he read the contents.

"We had no idea about any of this, of course," he admitted after finishing the letter. "The message we received was not very clear. We understood only that you were going to be heading this way. The rest of it was drowned out by interference."

Kellar started to slump forward, sounds of pain escaping his pale lips.

"We have a camp near here," the man said, sympathy entering his voice. "We shall do what we can."

The camp was underground, with men living in natural tunnels that were reached through caves in the side of the mountain range that dominated that area and extended into Switzerland, to become part of the Alpine group.

"It was wonderful to find all this," the leader, who had identified himself as Oskar Snyder, told Stephen Bartlett. "The SS seems blissfully unaware that it exists, a network of hiding places right under their feet."

"How far does it extend?" the American asked.

"To within several hundred yards of Dachau," Snyder said, then realized what Bartlett was getting at, and added, "But that is not close enough, I am afraid. The truth is that, before we ever reached the gates, we all would be slaughtered. The tunnels get us only so near, then we reach a dead end."

He nodded toward Felix Kellar and Gustav Dobrik, who were being held at the opposite end of a large cavern that seemed every bit as big as a football stadium.

"Even so, this network of tunnels gives us quite unrestricted movement for some distance . . . yet they remain valuable to us only so long as their existence goes undiscovered by the Nazis. Until now, nobody but the group of us here has known about this remarkable discovery . . . however, at this very moment, *they* do!" he said, jerking his head toward Kellar and Dobrik. "It is information that could destroy if it is ever leaked to the SS or the Gestapo!"

Bartlett saw the contempt that Snyder had for the two men.

"Neither of them is a National Socialist," he pointed out.

"They serve the aims of the Nazis just the same. What is the difference if they are members or not? If someone shoots my mother or my wife or my son in the back of the head, he is my enemy regardless of his political affiliation!"

Snyder was of medium height, with large shoulders that seemed disproportionate to the rest of his body. A large mustache extended from one end of his lip to the other. He had a wide, jagged scar that ran from just below his right earlobe to his dimpled chin.

"You notice my scar," he said as he saw Bartlett's gaze.

"Sorry . . ."

"No need to be. It is quite a topic of conversation. I nearly bled to death because of the wound that caused it. You see, I escaped from Auschwitz last year. My cheek was caught on some barbed wire."

Bartlett grimaced.

"The men who took care of me were not skilled in such matters," Snyder went on. "I suppose, now, that I shall never achieve my childhood dream of working in the German motion picture industry."

He chuckled a bit, then any humor vanished.

"They cannot live, you know," he said, nodding in the direction of Kellar and Dobrik. "Whatever my sympathy earlier for the wounded one's plight, I have to say that he is as much a danger as the others."

"But you read the letter from Rommel!" Bartlett protested.

"Sit down, Stephen," Snyder remarked. "You are overwrought right now. You are blinding yourself to reality."

"*Reality* is that both, however uncomfortable a prospect it is, want to help us."

"No, no, my American friend, reality is not what is written on a single sheet of crumpled paper from the hand of Germany's most celebrated war hero, delivered to us by a man who participated in the loathsome activities of *Kristallnacht*. That was when *real* tribulation for my people began, you know."

Bartlett knew nothing about Kellar's activities. He winced at memories of what he had learned about the Night of the Broken Glass.

"But I think he regrets whatever it was he did," he persisted. "This man's conscience is telling him to—"

"Nonsense," Snyder grunted. "His life is in our hands. What would you *expect* him to tell you, Stephen? Your *naiveté* is not endearing, I assure you."

Bartlett started to say something else but the other man held up his hand, palm outward, and signaled that there was no possibility of further discussion.

"Unacceptable," Bartlett said, jumping to his feet, angered by what he was being told.

As Snyder stood also, he stared straight at the other man and added, "You are not in charge here. If you want our assistance in freeing your loved ones from Dachau, you will put aside your ivory-tower morality."

Without further comment, he pulled out a pistol from a holster strapped to his waist and strode toward the two captives. When he was only a few feet away, he aimed the weapon at Dobrik's chest.

Bartlett had followed him and now lunged forward, knocking Snyder off his feet. Two of the partisans grabbed the American and dragged him to one side.

"You cannot do this!" Bartlett screamed.

"I am a Jew!" Snyder shot back. "I have *earned* the right to murder my enemies!"

"You cannot kill an unarmed prisoner, a man who *wants* to change," Bartlett shouted.

"His kind have sought the annihilation of my people."

"His *kind*, yes! But how could you *know* that *he* did any of that? Should all Jews be painted with the same dirty brush because of one dishonest financier ten years ago who profited from your country's troubles at the time, sending his minions into the nation's banking system to drain it of any wealth that remained?"

"You use Nazi stereotypes!"

"You have just threatened a man's life because of *Jewish* stereotypes, Oskar!"

Snyder had raised the handle of his pistol, intending to break Bartlett's jaw with it but now he wavered, looking over his shoulder at the terrified Felix Kellar.

"We open ourselves to betrayal," he said, hesitating, "if we are uncertain about his motives, about *anything* he may tell us."

"But with that man's help, we have someone well known in Nazi circles. He would be greeted with no suspicion if he were to gain entrance to Dachau."

"You are thinking only of your wife and son."

"There are tens of thousands of Jewish wives and sons in that camp. If Felix can help at all, how many of *them* could be freed?"

"Should we save his life now, will he be willing to lose it later?"

Kellar's voice, strained, weak, interrupted them.

"The tunnels . . . ," he said. "You . . . can . . . use . . . the . . . tunnels."

"You have been listening well," Snyder said sarcastically. "As you undoubtedly realize from what I said a moment ago, the tunnels *end* quite a distance away from the camp itself. We would have to charge into a clearing, with no cover to shield us. We would be massacred in minutes. But then that would hardly displease you, I am sure."

"You . . . are . . . very . . . wrong," Kellar persisted, though any strength he had was quickly dissipating.

"We are *not* wrong," Snyder spit out the words. "We have surveyed the area. The tunnels come right up against a solid wall of earth and stone."

"And . . . then . . . continue . . . on . . . *under* . . . Dachau!" Kellar added just before unconsciousness claimed him.

Snyder froze.

"If that is true," Bartlett broke in, "do you know what it means? Can you imagine what could be accomplished, Oskar?"

Slowly, almost reluctantly, Snyder nodded.

"Yes . . . ," he murmured. "Yes, I know."

He replaced the pistol in its holster.

"*If* this willing servant of a demonic regime is telling the truth . . . ," he spoke, his voice hardly above a whisper. Emotions playing across his face, he glanced back at Bartlett, and added, "We can only pray to Almighty God that he is."

12

J ews bankrupted my family and cast me out on the street," Felix Kellar was saying. "They descended like ravenous vultures upon all of Germany and were picking our bones clean until Adolf Hitler stepped onto the scene and sent them running. That was why I decided to become a National Socialist, to do the bidding of devils who were disguising themselves as angels bent on the redemption of the Fatherland!"

That was part of what Kellar told them when he regained consciousness after being given extraordinary medical care later that day by one of the newly arrived partisans, a prominent doctor from Frankfurt named Isidore Greisman. Kellar's anti-Semitic bias gave way, after a bit, to a stirring explanation of why his views had softened considerably over the past several years, a vivid outpouring of emotion that even suspicious, cynical resistance fighters found affecting.

Nevertheless, the delay caused a different kind of agony for Stephen Bartlett for it meant that much more time letting Lina Heydrich have her way with his wife and his son, and not knowing what he would find if he ever made it to Dachau.

"I know that the more information we can get out of Kellar, the better our chances are of being successful," he admitted as he and Oskar Snyder paused at the mouth of the secret cave. "But it is so hard, having no idea what is happening to them."

"Or once you think about it, *imagining* what might be going on," Snyder sympathized. "I have no one left, Stephen. These men here are my only family."

He sighed, then shook his head several times.

"You think I overreact when it comes to treating prisoners like those two and the other men, but in a war such as this, we become more and more like our enemy in so many respects because we have to think like them in order to be effective *against* them. Any principles of honor, dignity, or decency are the first casualties."

Bartlett grunted agreement, knowing from his own experience how accurate that declaration was.

"We bomb their cities and count it victorious when we reduce their buildings to rubble," Snyder added. "But when *they* attack London, we call them devils. Their innocent women and children can die by the thousands and we turn away, calling it merely 'unfortunate.' But when *ours* are ground to pulp amidst the rubble, it is an atrocity."

Bartlett looked at Snyder.

"I know what you are saying, Oskar," he said, "but there seems to be no other way. We act like rampaging jungle beasts in the process of waging war and end up being called heroes."

Snyder held out both hands in front of him.

"With these hands I have broken the necks of more men than I can remember. I have gutted countless others and . . . and . . ."

His hands were suddenly shaking.

"Still I manage somehow to sleep well at night," he went on. "How can that be, Stephen? The guards at the camps, I am told, sleep quite soundly. I myself have no nightmares, never did. I do not suddenly see myself covered with the blood of others and awaken, screaming, in the middle of the night.

"And I go on killing. The more dead each day the better I feel. Pieces of bodies are scattered through the air because of bombs I helped construct then plant, and I shout with celebration. We come back and have beers and sing our ballads of victory, and feel so satisfied."

"Reflex," Bartlett mumbled.

"What was that?" Snyder asked. "You are right . . . it's a conditioned reflex. After a while you can take your knife, wipe off the blade, and start to whistle a fine old ditty as you walk away from the body."

The American felt uncomfortable with such candid admissions but could not deny the truth of them.

"But what is the alternative, Oskar," Bartlett went on to pose the question, "to be so consumed with guilt that we can never kill again?"

He raised his left hand and pointed in the direction of Dachau.

"We are like surgeons, Oskar; think about that for a moment," he said.

Snyder was frowning as he tried to deal with what the American was telling him.

"Dachau represents the cancer. Our knives must cut into living flesh in order to get rid of it, hoping that we've gotten all that there is. But we must be *prepared* for more surgery, again and again, until there is no more cancer and the threat is gone forever."

Snyder shuddered.

"You have hit upon the problem, Stephen," he pointed out. "Explain . . ."

"In the German character there exists a *propensity* toward acts of savagery. We may well succeed today, tomorrow, next week, and, yes, ultimately win *this* war. Yet ten years from now, twenty, maybe thirty or forty or even fifty years from now, it will rise again, this Aryan hatred of anyone who is not racially pure."

Snyder cleared his throat.

"But there is something else, my friend," he said. "It is the Jewish people as a group. We Jews have viewed ourselves as doomed for so many centuries that when catastrophe actually does strike, as it has so often, we seem to have this suicidal tendency merely to submit to it as somehow our predestined fate."

"That is why there haven't been more uprisings," Bartlett mused.

"Entirely why. We seem to think, how do you say, we seem to think that it is our lot in life to die *en masse,* separated from our homeland forever. Thus, we ask, what is the sense of fighting back, and thereby aggravating our dilemma?"

"The trouble is that the Nazis probably realize this and trade upon it. Such an attitude is handing them an unholy advantage."

"Undoubtedly! I mean, how can I disagree with you? I have heard those butchers call us the Jewish version of lemmings. The only difference, they say, is that the pathetic little animals have straighter noses."

"But *you* fight. While others submit, you rise up against those who propose to annihilate you. What makes you different?"

"It is a complex matter, Stephen."

"Try me."

Snyder sighed with great weariness.

"Remember what Kellar said earlier?" he asked.

*Jews bankrupted my family and cast me out on the street . . .
they descended like ravenous vultures upon all of Germany and were
picking our bones clean until Adolf Hitler stepped onto the scene and
sent them running.*

"I do," Bartlett replied.

"My father was one of the financial experts, to be sure, a banker
to whom Kellar was referring. He *was* obsessed by money. It became
his god in a sense."

"The love of money . . ."

"Oh, yes, Stephen, that was it. My father proved to be everything Hitler used to justify his takeover of this country. My father
took homes away from people and cast them into the street without
compunction. Upon his word, families were ripped loose from everything they had known. The Great War did not destroy them—but
my father did."

"Yet you joined the resistance, Oskar. I would have thought
you would have become a Nazi instead."

"I tried, my friend, but they would not allow a Jew among
them, even a sympathetic one. I went so far as to point out that they
could use me for propaganda purposes but Goebbels would not hear
of it. He and the others turned their backs on me.

"I had no one, Stephen. I lived in the house of a man I came to
despise. And I could not join a movement that despised *me!*

"One day, it all changed for me. Goebbels ignored me, as I
said, in one way but apparently not another. All that I had told him
about my father became a part of the National Socialists' records.
When the time was right just two years ago, the black-shirts raided
our home and sent the entire family off to the camps.

"I shall never forget seeing my father's face, the skin so white
because shock had drained the blood from it. I had never told him
about my overtures to the Nazis but that last glimpse of him,
I . . . I thought I could see a look of bitter accusation crossing that
familiar face. Now I cannot stop wondering if he somehow had
learned the truth and kept it to himself, either hating me for
it . . . or forgiving me.

"I saw him again but only months later. After being shifted from
camp to camp, I ended up at Dachau. One night, unable to sleep, I
stood at the one window in that barracks-like building and saw a human skeleton walking down the dirt 'street' out front. Nearly all of his
bones were showing through his skin. There were bruises all over his
body. He was heading toward the nearest barbed-wire fence.

"A guard saw him, and ordered him to stop. He refused. Other guards emerged. Two of them dragged him back past the window. I could see his face. It was my father. They were taking him toward the ovens. I told myself that I could not allow this to happen without trying to help, to free him, even though it was likely that I, too, would die as a result.

"So I followed them, hoping I was being careful enough not to be detected. The guards approached the crematoriums. Usually it was only corpses that were placed inside. But this time it was someone barely alive—but alive nevertheless, the man who had given *me* life. They broke his arms and his legs as easily as thin tree branches so he could not move but only lie there as he was shoved into the oven.

"He seemed to turn again in my direction, seemed to be looking at me as before, this time not with accusation but with an expression of pity, not for himself but for me, as though he knew what monstrous guilt would be my lot throughout the rest of my days. He let out one scream—he had no strength for another—and then the flames took him!"

Snyder fell back against the mouth of the cave.

"I do not have nightmares from this, Stephen," he admitted. "I do not have nightmares about those I have killed along the way, after escaping from Dachau. I go to sleep at night. I awaken in the morning. I go about each day, one day after the other. I could slaughter the inhabitants of an entire village and still I would sleep.

"So it is, I am sure, with Himmler and Goebbels and Bormann and the Führer himself. I have become like my enemies, Stephen. *I have become like the men who sent my father into the ovens as I watched and did nothing!*"

Bartlett thought the other man was on the verge of collapse.

"You don't have to go on with this, Oskar," he offered. "You don't have to tell me anything more."

"But you need to know why I keep on killing. It is not so much the survival of my kind. I passed that point months ago. I kill the bastards because they are a mirror held before me, and in them I see only myself!"

He turned away.

"Would you go back inside?" he asked. "Would you tell those men they no longer have anything to fear from me?"

"I will, Oskar, I will."

"Thank you, Stephen. I will be in shortly."

As Bartlett was turning back inside, he heard Oskar Snyder say, "It is not the nights I loathe but the days. At night I rest, and there is oblivion for a few hours. During the day I do these terrible things in the name of liberation.

"It is the sunrise that I hate to face; God knows how true this is. I dread each awful day, the infamy in which I wallow, folding my hands of blood in prayer to Almighty God to end the misery of this my life."

The next morning, Felix Kellar had revived enough to tell Bartlett and Snyder what he had learned about Dachau.

"You will have only one chance," he was saying, his voice somewhat stronger. "Once the existence of the tunnels is known to the SS, you can be sure all steps will be taken to seal them off permanently."

He paused, catching his breath, then continued, "I found out when I visited the camp last year. I had never been to one before, you know. They say Himmler hasn't either, though I wonder how believable that is.

"There is some suspicion that, if it is true, Himmler is putting off any such encounter because he has softened a bit and is hardly eager to see the results of his policy toward the Jews."

"Himmler, softening?" Snyder spat out the words. "Are you mad?"

"No, Snyder, I am not," Kellar replied, bristling. "It is easy to get into a situation where orders are issued that we must obey and yet we somehow remain detached from their effect. *Saying* that a million Jews should be destroyed is one thing. It is quite another to look at them in ditches, piled high, or in ovens or newly gassed."

"But Himmler is not an isolated, insignificant bureaucrat who has never been out in the real world," Snyder reminded him. "You do not expect me to believe that he is somehow naive about all of this."

"That is not what I am trying to say," Kellar replied. "I can only speak to you with any validity about what it did to me. For some time I had been disillusioned. For some time I questioned in my own brain the morality of official policy. Like so many others, I had been determined to obey those who were my superiors. But being at Dachau was one of two events that made my questions all the more insistent."

"What was the other?"

"Frau Heydrich's need for vengeance, even if this meant sacrificing the life of a man like Field Marshal Rommel."

"In other words, piles of Jew bodies were not enough!" Snyder blurted, spittle hitting the air in front of his mouth. "Is that what you are saying? But woe to anyone who dared to assault a single German officer!"

Kellar was sitting up on a makeshift bed. He bowed his head, groaning a bit.

"That is to my shame, yes," he agreed. "But I was simply living out my heritage. I was brought up by Aryan parents who clung to the myth of our superiority over all races. I carried with me the hatred they felt because I refused to doubt their beliefs and cast them aside. I loved them deeply and would not shame them in that manner."

Snyder had been sitting in front of the other man. Now he stood, his face reddening with deep anger.

"Despite your so-called *shame*, you nevertheless attacked that house. You pushed your conscience aside."

"Of that I am guilty," Kellar agreed. "I do not know if I am ever to be forgiven but I pray that you will realize how I *now* feel: I would rather die than give another day more to those monsters in Berlin."

A few seconds passed.

No one spoke.

Then Snyder swung around and faced Felix Kellar, but not before a visible shudder gripped his body.

"No need to tell us anything else," he said. "We both are guilty, you know. We have dipped our guilty hands in the life-force of other human beings, and our souls will carry the stain with us to the grave—and perhaps beyond."

13

The network of tunnels extended for more than thirty miles toward Dachau and in other directions, coming quite close to Natzweiler and Flossenburg as well, the latter a camp that, like Dachau, was a center for medical experiments.

"If only we had enough men, we could raid three camps at the same time!" Snyder exclaimed. "But there is never a sufficient cache of armaments or men to do all that we would like to accomplish."

Both he and Bartlett were sitting in the main tunnel area, looking into the darkness just ahead of them.

"Have we an impossible task here, Stephen?" Snyder asked.

"I cannot say if we do or not," Bartlett replied. "I know only one thing: My wife and my son are there. A madman will be seeing them soon, if he hasn't already. When I think of what he might do, I realize that, whatever the cost, I could not stop trying to free them."

"Both your people and mine suffer the wrath, one and the same," Snyder added, "Jew and Gentile together under the sword of Satan!"

After they had emerged from the tunnel and were standing in the main cavern again, Snyder told the American, "There is another entrance some miles ahead. I think the closer we can get before going underground the better."

"Why?" Bartlett asked. "I don't understand your reasoning, Oskar. I thought the tunnel system was a perfect natural barrier to being discovered. Aboveground, there is plenty of opportunity for a mishap."

"Some parts of it collapse from time to time, Stephen. Heavy equipment rolls over the tunnels, sometimes daily. We could make all the maps we wanted but they might well be outdated within twenty-four hours as new trucks and tanks and whatever else precipitate more cave-ins. You mustn't forget that ours is a wet country, and the ground is often quite soft, even spongy, which makes it all the more susceptible to collapse."

"Then this could happen while we are underground."

"It could, my friend, it could. But there is no other choice. Trying to get at Dachau otherwise would be suicidal, as you must know by now."

Bartlett nodded as he said, "Forgive me, Oskar. I think of that camp and I don't see tens of thousands of helpless prisoners or your men at all, I just see one woman and one boy I love very much."

"We start tonight," Snyder said.

"Is Dobrik going with us?"

"He is not. I am keeping him right here, under guard, along with Kellar's men, until all this is over. Besides, his foot will take some time to heal. For his own sake, he is better off not subjecting it to heavy activity."

"What about afterward?"

"I cannot say. I mean, can you seriously suggest that, somehow, I should bring myself to trust the man?"

"You seem inclined to trust Kellar."

"He told us about those tunnels under Dachau. He gave us valuable information that we can use. However, this Dobrik character has done nothing of the sort. Are you so sure about him yourself?"

Bartlett had to admit he wasn't.

But our cause is . . . the total elimination of any and all Jew scum from German soil.

Dobrik had never recanted, whatever personal admiration he might have developed for Bartlett himself.

"What time tonight?" Bartlett asked.

"Just before midnight," Snyder replied. "Fortunately there will be no full moon. We will have a maximum cover of darkness to hide us."

Bartlett bowed his head in a momentary prayer. When he was finished and looked up again, the other man asked, "For your loved ones?"

"Yes. We are so close to the two of them now, and yet they might as well be on another planet."

"A dark and inhospitable one at that," Snyder agreed, placing his hand on the American's shoulder.

Field Marshal Erwin Rommel had reached Berlin and had been given an immediate meeting with Heinrich Himmler.

"You are looking well," Himmler said in his usual colorless manner.

"Thank you, Heinrich," replied Rommel. "I have an urgent need to discuss."

"The attempt to assassinate you?"

Rommel knew he had to choose his words with the greatest delicacy.

"I do not as yet have very many facts," he said.

"But I do. I suspect it was Reinhard's widow," Himmler replied.

Rommel knew that feigning surprise would not work with this man, for he was able, quickly, to see through such pretense.

"The American suspected as much," he said simply.

"This action was hardly a complete disaster then? Stephen Bartlett, I must assume, is dead. Am I not correct?"

"In fact, he may not be, Heinrich."

Himmler had been sitting behind his desk, toying with a thin-bladed knife that he used as a letter-opener. Abruptly he froze.

"Where would he be if he were not dead, Erwin?" he asked in a monotone.

"I sent him away with my men to guard him."

Himmler's face flared red.

"You had the murderer of Reinhard Heydrich in your presence and you let him *go*?" he roared. "How can you *ever* justify that?"

Rommel knew that caution was now pointless.

"Because Heydrich was a monster!" he declared. "He epitomized a national policy running amuck!"

Himmler dropped the knife and slammed his fist down on the desk.

"You border on treason!" he said, trying to control himself.

"Were you aware of the fact that he was plotting to have *you* murdered?" Rommel threw the revelation at him.

"Not possible," Himmler retorted. "Not—"

Rommel reached into his jacket and pulled out a small envelope. On the back was a seal that marked it TOP SECRET.

"Read it," he interrupted. "Read it, and then tell me you still believe in your protégé's loyalty."

Himmler broke the seal and pulled a single sheet of paper from the envelope. Beads of perspiration appeared on his forehead as he read the contents.

After he had finished, he said nothing for a moment or two.

"What does this have to do with the American?" he asked, trying to keep his voice from betraying his emotions.

Rommel leaned forward.

"It could be said, Heinrich, that you are sitting in that chair today because the American and his colleagues *succeeded!*"

Himmler's slender, pale, almost girlishly soft hands, covered with blue veins so close to the surface that they stood out with striking visibility, hands that had been tapping lightly on the desktop, abruptly went limp, like a rag doll's.

"Did the widow approach you about helping?" Rommel asked, sensing another reason for the man's discomfort.

"Yes . . . ," Himmler replied.

"And you rejected her request."

No answer.

"So Lina Heydrich went ahead entirely on her own, is that it? Ignoring your wishes in the process?"

Himmler grunted another yes.

"That seems to say that she held nothing but contempt for you."

"Be very careful. Your status as a hero may not shield you in *every* situation."

"Thank you for reminding me. The lessons of a few hours ago were not enough."

Inexplicably, Himmler broke out laughing for a few seconds; there was little real humor in it, yet seeing the cold, stern architect of the Final Solution reacting in this manner startled Rommel.

"You must never tell anyone I laughed," Himmler said after he had stopped. "They would either think you a liar or call me mad."

"No one will hear it from my lips," Rommel assured him.

Himmler leaned forward, his elbows on the desk.

"I will help," the second most powerful man in the Nazi regime said. The slightest hint of a mischievous smile crossed the face that could have belonged to a harmless, owlish schoolteacher, with his gray-blue eyes, neatly trimmed mustache below a perfectly shaped nose, and, finally, his thin lips and receding chin. Surely this was the face of a man given to intelligence and introspection, not the ordering of mindless violence against innocent millions.

Rommel was prepared for a longer discussion, one marked by at least a few more outbursts of anger between them.

"That surprises you," Himmler observed of the other man's expression.

Rommel had to agree that it did.

"Can you suppose there could be a single instant of humanity in one whom so many have thought to be a child of the Devil himself?" Himmler asked, his voice uncharacteristically bordering on being tender.

"We are in a war," Rommel replied noncommittally. "There are times when we all act like animals, I suppose."

"Or when animals seem almost human, eh?"

Rommel reached for the phone on his desk.

"Get me whoever is in charge of *Sonderbehandlung* at Dachau," he spoke crisply into the receiver, then listened for a moment.

He hung up and turned toward Rommel.

"The lines are down," he said. "The camp cannot be reached by wire. We shall have to leave for Dachau immediately."

"*You* are going, Heinrich?" Rommel asked, stunned.

"Even the Desert Fox cannot overturn *my* orders, my dear Erwin."

"The widow may be there."

"I know her well," Himmler assured him. "You might say that I am familiar with every inch of her."

Rommel's eyebrows shot up, but he said nothing.

"There was a time when my bed was more enticing to her than that of the man whose memory has inspired her passionate feelings of vengeance," Heinrich Himmler said, a knowing smirk on his face. "This new lust of widow Heydrich's for the blood of Stephen Bartlett and his family is not the only one she has been guilty of in recent years."

14

The tunnel seemed little different from the one connected to the house where Field Marshal Erwin Rommel had taken him.

They had reached it after traveling over tree- and rock-strewn terrain that caused stress to vehicles that already seemed on the verge of collapse, battered and rusty cars and trucks that in better times would have been consigned to scrap-metal heaps.

"Are these found throughout this entire region?" Bartlett asked as he stood before another cave some fifteen miles away from the one the partisans had made their headquarters.

"It is honeycombed with them," Snyder assured him. "Amazingly, the Nazis have no idea about what exists right beneath their feet. The military implications are devastating. If, someday, we are able to organize operations properly and get the Allied support we need, well, we could literally pull the ground out from beneath these monsters."

"You have a map concentrating on the tunnels' relationship to the camps," the American inquired. "But what about military installations? Is there some possibility of an underground offensive against any of those?"

"We are working on that, Stephen. All of this is very new to us, of course. You have to remember, my friend, that because we are *Jewish* partisans, none of us have come from the military. We are primarily educators, farmers, accountants, lawyers by profession. And we have only limited resources at present."

"From what I've seen," Bartlett told him, "you can be sure that the Allies will want to work with you."

Five dozen men had gathered at this newest cave entrance, deliberately making the trip in battered old cars and trucks from widely disparate locations, to avoid causing suspicion. There was no curfew in effect as yet in the countryside, only in cities such as Berlin, Frankfurt, Dusseldorf, and others, though the driver of each vehicle had to be ready with a seemingly reasonable explanation for his nighttime travel just in case he happened to be stopped by a Nazi patrol.

"Fortunately, by their very nature, all of these caves are in the remotest possible regions," Snyder added. "Also, the Nazis seem to concentrate their patrols on the well-traveled roads, oblivious to what is happening off the beaten track.

"But I cannot suppose their ignorance will last forever. Someday a patrol might stumble upon part of the network of tunnels; someday a traitor might leak to the Gestapo what we have here. We must do what we can while we are the only ones aware of all this."

They were less than five miles from Dachau.

Kellar had drawn a rough map for them, in addition to providing the poignant reason why he never told the commandant of Dachau what had happened.

"As I said earlier, I had never been to a camp before," he recalled. "I had heard the stories, yes, but tended not to believe most of them, assuming they were nothing more than Allied or partisan-inspired propaganda. I no longer clung to the delusion that the war was a righteous one but I had not, then, allowed myself to see that it was little more than a brutal facade for the insane actions of some unbalanced fanatics."

Still quite weak, Kellar had paused for several minutes while sipping some brandy to relieve the pain that continued to hammer his body.

"No one who visits one of the camps for the first time can come away from the experience without his emotions being affected," he continued. "And those who must stay, such as the guards, the ones who are not sadists to begin with, either are corrupted by what happens or they become secret alcoholics in order to dull whatever consciences they have left. When the war is over, I will be interested to see what statistics become available to see how many of the guards die of alcohol-related ailments."

"But how did you find out about the tunnel system?" Snyder asked, not entirely letting go of his suspicions about the man.

"Some of the prisoners had been digging a tunnel of their own when they ran into it," Kellar answered.

"So you turned them in and sealed up what they had started?"

"I did *not!*" Kellar retorted, irritated at the lingering distrust that was evident in Snyder's cynical tone of voice. "Should I be as uncertain of your intentions as you are about mine, I would be telling you none of this!"

Snyder nodded, adding, "You are right. I look at you as a German, and I think only the darkest thoughts. Please forgive me, Felix."

Kellar went on to tell them he was near one of the housing units when he heard some crying and screaming. When he rushed inside, a group of Jews looked up from their digging, startled that they had been found out.

"I had arrived at Dachau only hours before, and had not had much contact with those confined to it. It was night, and I was on the way to my temporary quarters."

"What *did* you do?" Bartlett asked.

They had seemed little more than walking corpses, these pathetic men. Their fingers were bloody from digging through to the tunnel.

Kellar had raised his pistol, ready to fire it.

"I froze as I saw them—or what was left of them," he continued. "They were so pale, thin, the outlines of their ribs visible. Some were coughing; others were simply breathing heavily. Each had bloodshot eyes, eyes that seemed to protrude nearly all the way out of their sockets. A few were naked, the rest wore only the thinnest rags."

He looked from Snyder to Bartlett to the other partisans who had gathered nearby, listening to his story.

"They expected me to shoot them right there or else to immediately sound an alarm and have others do such a deed for me," Kellar said. "They seemed almost to be *asking* for this. If they could not escape in that manner, they would gladly do so another way, through death at the end of a rifle or a pistol."

But he could neither kill them himself nor get others to take over. What he had done instead stunned the men whose attention he now held so completely in that large cavern.

"I told them they would be all right, that I would not expose their plan. Not only that, I said I would help them. I would arrange for someone to be on the other end of the tunnel, someone who could be trusted, someone who would hide them away, nurse them back to health, and then try to get them across the border into Switzerland. But a few had to remain in order to patch the entrance so nothing could be discovered."

"What happened?" Snyder asked.

"They went into the tunnel. The others sealed up the entrance in their building and reset the wooden planks over it. But the men never emerged from the other end. I had someone waiting for them, but they just did not come out. They are still inside, either killed by a cave-in or by their own physical condition or both. Their bodies have been there all this time."

"How did you get a map then?" Bartlett interjected.

"The prisoners who remained behind to cover up the tunnel entrance gave it to me as best they could. But it *is* far from complete. It shows only a small part of the network; or there may be no more tunnels after all. Who can say? I know only about that one area."

"If they knew about it, why had they not tried to escape before?" Snyder asked.

"They did," Kellar replied.

"What stopped them?"

"Gas."

"Gas?" Snyder questioned. "The Nazis flooded the tunnel with gas? That means they *did* know about it. I thought you said—"

"You jump to conclusions," Kellar interrupted. "It was gas from one of the so-called *brausebaders* at Dachau. It leaked into the tunnels through cracks in the ground. Several of the prisoners died as they tried to escape. Their bodies were simply left behind. But as the terrors at the camp increased, the other men realized they would *have* to take another chance, for if they were to stay, death was nothing less than certain."

"That was the night when you happened upon them . . . ," Snyder spoke, not unsympathetically this time.

Kellar nodded as he said, "Afterward, I was able to find out the schedule at the *brausebaders,* which were not kept in operation day and night. There were several periods when they simply were idle, though the walls continued to reek of hydrocyanic acid fumes."

He could not talk much longer, his voice becoming progressively weaker.

"Let me add this: I tried very hard to save them. I did what I could. I have no idea why the second group did not make it out. Perhaps they were simply too old, too sick, too weak to endure. But there was no other way."

"You ran quite a risk," Bartlett observed, not hiding the degree of admiration he had begun to feel for the man.

"But, you see, I never considered my conduct as traitorous to my government. Rather, I believed I was helping some poor souls avoid death, death that no human being deserved. It was a humanitarian impulse on my part, nothing more, nothing less."

The group's plan was to travel the remaining distance by foot in the tunnel system itself. One man would remain behind for each of the vehicles so they could be scattered in different, prearranged locations. Leaving them in that one spot would only draw attention to the fact that there was something special about that particular cave.

Making connections again with their transportation could be quite another problem, the men realized. They did not take any radio transmitters with them for fear they would be intercepted. It was decided that four men would be stationed around Dachau, each with binoculars, looking at the camp from a different angle and constantly alert to what was going on. Once they saw any indication that the break-in had occurred, they could return to the cars and trucks and be ready for the escaping partisans and prisoners alike.

The tunnels were more than six feet high and three times as wide. Walking through them was not difficult. But there were frequent slippery patches of mud not always discernible in the beams of their flashlights or lanterns. Just two miles from their destination, they were tired and dirty but realized that the hardest task would soon face them:

Breaking through the wall of dirt that separated them from the portion of the tunnel system *under* Dachau.

The prisoners who had earlier come up against it had been so wasted by months of malnutrition and disease that all they had to show for their efforts to dug through it were bloody fingertips. Snyder had seen to it that his men were far better equipped. They carried with them, in addition to weapons, pickaxes and shovels.

As soon as they reached the wall, they started hacking away at it, four men at a time, until their strength was dispelled; then five more replaced them, and so it went.

Bartlett and Snyder sat farther back in the tunnel in a conveniently wider section where most of the other men were waiting along with them. They went over the details of their plan yet again, trying to see if they had missed anything.

They would wait underground until just before midnight, then break through at the spot Kellar had suggested, which was under a building where prisoners were crammed in particularly tight. One by one, these poor souls would be helped down into the tunnel opening. Those who were able to use weapons would be given pistols. Once that building was emptied, the partisans planned to use it as a temporary command center.

Some would remain inside that building while the others reentered the tunnel and used it to get to a few of the other buildings with prisoners. As many as possible would be hurried underground. The rest needed to remain where they were, some armed with guns, others with grenades, a few with knifes. The tunnels could not hold an unlimited number of people, and the selection process had to be quick and arbitrary, with one exception: the men who seemed closer to death would not be sent into the tunnels. This plan seemed cruel when it was decided upon, but Snyder, Bartlett, and the others realized there was no other choice. Navigating the tunnels was arduous work. The truly weak, the ones who were obviously dying, would never make it, and the limited space involved could not be allowed to clog up with corpses.

Bartlett shuddered as he went over that reasoning, not relishing the sight of tortured men looking at him with obvious pain as they saw their comrades being given a chance to leave while they had to remain behind.

"The dirty work is just ahead, but it is necessary," Snyder was saying. "However, we all await that moment when we can break out and attack. We have been praying for an opportunity such as this for a long time."

The others, hearing this, murmured agreement.

Natalie and Andrew, Bartlett thought. *Kellar assumed they were being held in separate quarters since undoubtedly they would be prepared separately for whatever treatment Mengele decided to inflict upon them. He felt sure that Lina Heydrich would want to be present to witness everything. Where those quarters were located could not be pinned down conclusively, but Kellar thought the best guess might be a small room adjacent to the medical research building.*

He suddenly felt queasy. What would he encounter if he did find his family? Were they alive? Would they be in such condition that death was the better choice? Would he find his beloved Natalie floating in a tank of near-freezing water? Or had Andrew already been subjected to some grotesque transplant experiment?

Months earlier, he had read an intelligence report that said Mengele was keenly interested in exploring the possibility of brain transplants!

He had started to fall asleep, his head tipping over toward his chest, but that hideous image jolted him back to full consciousness. He grunted as if kicked.

"Stephen, are you ill, my friend?" Snyder asked.

"No," he replied, "just thinking about my family and wondering what shape they will be in."

"Are you prepared for *whatever* you might find, even the worst?"

Bartlett sucked in his breath.

"I doubt it," he admitted.

"You can let nothing spoil the plan," Snyder reminded him.

"I realize that. The Nazis must not be allowed any clue as to what is going on."

"You may want to go on the rampage, Stephen, if you find out something terrible about your wife and your son. Your emotions will try to take over. But you must control that urge."

"I *do* know that!" Bartlett said angrily.

Snyder grabbed the American's wrist.

"It is not just *your* family," he said. "Thousands of families are involved. I am not being insensitive when I remind you of what is at stake here."

Bartlett saw the expression on the other man's face, and nodded.

"You live with this kind of pressure every day," Bartlett commented. "I do not."

"It is not something one gets used to," Snyder said. "I am just trying to prepare you, Stephen. The images you have gotten of places like Dachau have been from espionage film clips or on printed newspaper or magazine pages. I have been there in person. I have seen the depths of this evil place, smelled it, tasted the polluted water, eaten food crawling with worms.

"When I was at Dachau, the experiments had just started. I remained long enough to witness what was left of bodies that were carted out of the laboratory building."

"How *did* you get out?" Bartlett asked.

Snyder's face lost any color that it had left.

"When no one was looking, I threw myself on the cart they used for corpses," he said, each word steeped in pain. "I was dumped into a pit with the others. The guards never knew. I *looked* as bad as the rest. I was prepared to claw my way through the dirt mixed with lime that I expected them to throw on top of the bodies. I waited.

Oh, Stephen, that wait seemed hours long but it could only have been minutes. I heard someone say, 'Wait. There are more. We have plenty of room. Let's go back and get them.

"I had to push my way through a layer of bodies to get to the edge of that stinking, unholy pit. Then I pulled myself over the top. Can you conceive what that was like, my friend? Can you understand what it does to a man's mind, yes, to his soul?"

He waved an arm toward the other men sitting nearby.

"These men found me and took me in and nursed me back from the abyss," he said, smiling a bit. "They are my family now, my life."

He hesitated, then added, "I know what you are feeling, Stephen. You see, a member of my own family somehow may still be there in Dachau. My mother was not dead when I escaped. She wanted to be, because the separation from my father was as bad as the rest of the nightmare there. But she could not take her own life; so she hung on, doing what good she could for the others and herself."

He looked toward the ceiling of the tunnel.

"I hope my mother is *not* alive," he whispered, "for she would be better off having died a long time ago. I mean, what could be left of this woman, Stephen, after so long in hell?"

An hour or so later, the group was confronted by the wall of stone and dirt that had stopped them in the past, forcing them to assume that the tunnel actually ended at that point. But now they knew what was on the other side.

"There is no way of telling how thick this section may be," Snyder observed, "or how long it will take us to get through to the other end. Whatever the case, we have little time to waste. And remember, please, that we have to work as quietly as possible."

He paused after making that last statement, seemed to be considering it for a moment, and then added somewhat defensively, "*Could* the Nazis hear us aboveground? Who can say? But we mustn't take any sort of chance. More important, and more likely, noise can cause vibration, and it is perhaps even more of a danger that we all might be buried by a cave-in and suffocate right beneath their feet!"

Everyone grunted agreement, and then the work commenced with small axes and shovels being used by just a few men at a time in shifts of half an hour each, the preceding group going back in the line to rest as others took their place.

Snyder noticed that Bartlett, who was not in the work detail, was sweating, and seemed increasingly nervous.

"Have you a cold? A fever?" he asked.

"Claustrophobia is something of a problem for me," the American confessed, shivering. "Yet it's never been crippling, Oskar . . . just something I've learned to control in surroundings such as we have here."

"Along with hordes of black snakes, I imagine."

"What was that?" Bartlett reacted sharply, startled that the other man actually knew this about him.

"I heard you mumbling in your sleep the other night, Stephen. You apparently had an encounter in another tunnel not so far from here."

Embarrassed, Bartlett said nothing.

"It's okay, my friend," Snyder spoke reassuringly. "Only Jesus Christ was perfect—according to your theology anyway."

Bartlett would have liked to pursue the opening for discussion that comment represented, but he was cut off by the sound of someone screaming directly ahead.

Startled, the two men stood, then hurried to the digging site.

They stopped short when they saw what had startled one of the men.

A human skeleton.

Partially obscured by dirt was a human skeleton raggedly clothed in a pair of flimsy pajamas, the standard garb for concentration-camp prisoners.

The one who had unearthed the skeleton was standing by himself, leaning on the handle of a shovel.

"Please, forgive me!" he exclaimed. "I know that was careless, yelling as I did. But . . . but I couldn't help myself, Oskar. Whoever it was wanted freedom, and he got another kind of grave instead."

As he pointed toward the ceiling, he whispered, "I pray to Almighty God that no one up there heard me."

At first Snyder was angry but, recognizing how natural such a response was, he smiled reassuringly and told the man and the three others standing nearby to continue.

"But what about that?" one of them asked, pointing to the skeleton.

ROGER ELWOOD

"We can do nothing for the moment," Snyder replied. "After all, what is the alternative? Bury him somewhere else? What we must concentrate on is making sure some of those still alive escape this same fate."

Bartlett and Snyder went back to their spots at the end of the line of partisans waiting to pitch in as diggers.

"It's going to become much worse, you know," Bartlett told him. "There may be dozens of other bodies just ahead."

Snyder nodded reluctantly.

"The men are prepared now, as much as they can be." He spoke with what seemed like forced self-assurance. "They have some idea of what to expect. I doubt that we have to worry about another such outburst."

He was wrong.

As the final foot of dirt and rock crumbled and the partisans got through to the open tunnel beyond it, they saw what everyone knew awaited them. Still, that didn't help mitigate the horror they now witnessed.

Scores of skeletons, not just a random one or two.

Pile after pile of them.

Most were on their backs or sides, partially covered by dirt, but a few seemed to be half-standing, frozen in that position, their hands reaching out as though trying to push something away from them.

These were the ones who died from breathing the poisonous fumes of what had come to be known as Zyklon-B.

And just not adults.

A number of the skeletons were quite a bit smaller than the rest, obviously young children.

Bartlett himself made perhaps the most pathetic discovery.

A tiny form, not more than fourteen inches from head to foot.

"A baby!" the American exclaimed, picking it up with great care as tears rolled down his cheeks.

"It is one thing to *know* this happens, Stephen," Snyder reminded him, "but another altogether to hold the bones in your hands and realize what evil thing was done to a fine little child who once breathed the air of life, not the poison that entered his lungs down here!"

Soon the shock they all felt as they stood in that mass grave was being replaced by a heightened urgency to get on with what they had intended, freeing as many prisoners as possible . . . maybe even liberating the *entire* camp.

The rest of the way was clear, right up to where the original group of Dachau's prisoners had dug through to the tunnel.

"They must have had no idea that any of this existed," Bartlett mused. "Think of how they felt when they discovered it."

"Freedom, Stephen," Snyder said. "They thought only of freedom. They were so excited, my friend, filled with hope."

Soon the partisans arrived at the point where they thought the others had broken through from the building above.

"This *is* it, I think!" one of the men commented softly. "It seems to be precisely as we were told earlier!"

He stood back, looked at the spot for a moment, then nodded enthusiastically, and started to drive his pickax upward in a slow arc as carefully as he could, prepared to jump to one side if the dirt seemed especially loose.

Others joined in with him, saying nothing while they tried as a team to work as efficiently as possible.

Finally they hit the wooden floor above.

"We've made it!" they whispered in unison, ignoring the stench that drifted down through the planks.

Snyder told them, "Good! Break through. The prisoners must be asleep now, as much as they *can* sleep in this place. According to what Kellar told us, we should be right in the middle of the building."

They continued hacking away; demolishing the flimsy, rotting wood was an easy enough task after burrowing through the natural barrier behind them.

"Ugh," someone grunted. "That awful—!"

Abruptly the reason for the ever-stronger odor became apparent.

"Oh my G—!" Oskar Snyder started to exclaim as he caught a stark glimpse of what was happening.

The floor gave way in an instant, revealing a great, stinking mass of scores of relatively fresh human bodies, male and female alike, bodies that fell down upon them, a few still warm to the touch.

"*Leichenkeller!* We must be just below the—!" Snyder yelled an instant before he became partially submerged by this grisly discovery.

"Some . . . are . . . still . . . alive!" a dozen voices rose as a single, urgent whisper from the overwhelmed partisans.

Stephen Bartlett found himself gaping at an unclothed woman whose eyelids had suddenly flickered open a moment before she muttered in terror, her strained voice nearly inaudible, "Please . . . not the ovens . . . I live . . . I live . . . *not the ovens!*" Then she gasped once, suddenly limp against him.

Leichenkeller . . . not merely a dismal, unpainted building that housed several scores of tormented living human beings crowded together in wretched conditions of abysmal deprivation, but a place instead reserved momentarily for the recent dead.

Leichenkeller . . . the corpse cellars of Dachau.

15

Many of the men could not help screaming, despite knowing that any such sounds would bring SS guards to the building, but revulsion and shock made them unable to divorce their emotions from the sheer nightmare of that moment.

That was what happened . . . a sudden SS presence was heard as troopers stormed into the building above that section of the cellars, past the shovels, buckets, and other items used by other prisoners to bury the dead in mass graves near Dachau . . . and then up to the cellar's large double doors, which were quickly unlocked.

"Who knows what the Jews would do with these bodies when they get hungry?" one of the guards said, laughing harshly as he put the lock in his pocket and helped the others lift up the heavy doors. "They have the strangest appetites."

"But is human flesh kosher?" another added.

"No one can say what goes on in those Jew brains, especially when they are scrambling to fill their stomachs!"

More laughter.

Finally they stepped back as they saw what had happened.

The floor had collapsed, dozens of bodies plunging with it to the darkness below.

And movement among the cold, lifeless pile of flesh.

The guards had started to raise their weapons, but it was too late for some of them. Five died instantly as shots were leveled at them from the mass of bodies below. The others stepped back, ready to throw grenades into the opening.

"Only tear gas for the moment!" a woman's voice spoke harshly. "They are to be taken alive! Is that understood?"

The men disliked obeying orders from any woman but their superiors approved, so they had to do what they were told.

Tear-gas canisters were dropped into the opening and then the SS troopers hurried outside the building, and waited . . .

An instant later—

A terrible roar shuddered through the tunnel, shaking the ground and causing several of the corpses to tremble like marionettes in a pretense of life, with faint gray clouds of dust and loose earth stirred up as well.

Too soon, Stephen Bartlett thought, while he and the others tried clumsily to extricate themselves from that great mass of bodies; *it's as though they had been standing outside all along, primed for everything. And now that explosion, or whatever it was . . . part of a timetable carefully planned to greet us.*

"Tear gas!" he called frantically to the partisans as he staggered to his feet. "Back up farther into the tunnel!"

A handful had already bolted in that direction a minute or so before. But they started to return almost as quickly.

"Blocked!" came the shout. "It has been blocked. That was the explosion we heard. Everything's caved in behind us."

Trying to get his bearings, Bartlett suddenly glimpsed Snyder, lying prostrate near a rock. Blood was gathering in a pool beside his head, his eyes open, his mouth moving slowly, guttural sounds emerging from it.

Bartlett hurried to his side.

"Her name is Helena," Snyder managed to say. "If you come in contact with her, tell my beloved mother that I tried . . . that I tried so hard."

His head turned to one side. He gasped once and then he was limp, his eyes remaining open, a tear momentarily stationary on the edge of his left lower lid.

The rest of the partisans were pushing bodies aside, climbing out of the stinking morass that had submerged them. Though he was an American, not a German Jew, the men turned immediately to Bartlett instead of to one of their own.

"We are trapped!" one of the shorter partisans blurted out the obvious. "What should we do, Stephen?"

Bartlett felt uncomfortable taking over but realized that he had no choice. Leaving the men *without* a leader could prove disastrous.

"I heard a woman's voice," he said. "She spoke with such authority that I can only suppose that she has connived her way into being put in charge."

"That seems absurd, even for the Nazis," the same man retorted, aware of how macho the SS and Gestapo pretended to be while often covertly pursuing homosexual activity despite the official ban that Heinrich Himmler had imposed.

"This one woman is motivated by a personal obsession and she will stop at nothing to achieve what she wants."

"What *does* she want?"

"Me."

They started grumbling among themselves. A few stepped aside as a short, stocky, middle-aged man came forward.

"My name is Herman Scheinfeld," he said as he came forward. "You can be sure we *will* stand behind you."

Bartlett knew that he could conduct himself in a very noble manner before all the men and decline such a spirit of sacrifice, but the truth was that Lina Heydrich would never let any of the others off easily in any event, for they had gone on to *help* him, which in her mind was the unforgivable sin.

"It's clear . . . that we cannot . . . retreat," he told them, starting to cough more and more as the gas drifted into that section of the tunnel. "Our . . . escape route has been . . . conveniently removed. . . . Somehow they knew . . . what was going to . . . happen."

That caused more murmuring.

"It must have been Dobrik," Scheinfeld suggested. "Or Kellar."

"Not . . . Kellar."

Bartlett was scarcely able to speak now as the tear gas spread.

"Lie down," he shouted. "Play dead. . . . When they think we've . . . been knocked out . . . they may come . . . after . . . us . . . we . . . have to . . . be . . . ready!"

They started tearing off portions of their clothing and wetting them down from canteens strapped to their waists. They placed the rags over their noses and mouths as they sprawled on the hard, rocky ground.

Finally dozens of men could do nothing else except wait.

A hundred feet ahead of them, nearly a score of battered old flashlights rested on the ground wherever they had fallen, casting faint or strong beams in scattered directions, some illuminating in a bizarre jumble the pitiable, filthy mass of lifeless bodies cast down from that section of the *Leichenkeller*.

Gas-produced haze blurred sight, making the scene seem like a montage of dim visions from someone's surreal nightmare.

125

A thickening stench arose from the mixture of acrid chemicals and the sweat and blood from scores of abused and battered human bodies, along with the largely inescapable odor of deterioration that had already started to affect the lifeless bodies left unrefrigerated since they were brutalized hours earlier.

Flooding past the jagged edges of wood surrounding the gaping hole in the cellar floor were streaks of pale moonlight that made the dead faces, especially those with their eyelids frozen open, seem all the more ghostly, their thin, distorted shadows framed eerily by the sides and ceiling of the tunnel.

"Listen! I hear nothing!" someone whispered. "No more canisters. They've stopped throwing them down here. I wonder what . . ."

Silence. Total, except for their voices.

"Tormenting us," another added, "playing with us . . . they the cats and we the mice . . . and they are ready to pounce any time."

Minutes passed.

Still no more activity aboveground.

"Keep your weapons ready!" Bartlett urged.

And then—

Drilling.

Drilling sounds.

Scheinfeld started to speak, but Bartlett demanded that he be silent.

They're either behind us, he thought, *a contingent ready to break through, squeezing us from both sides or . . .*

He felt cold sweat drench his body.

Above.

His gaze darted toward the ceiling.

Heartbeat quickening, he guessed a possible explanation after remembering what had killed those earlier prisoners.

It was gas from one of the so-called brausebaders at Dachau. It leaked into the tunnels through cracks in the ground. Several of the prisoners died as they tried to escape. Their bodies were simply left behind.

Kellar had said this was an accident, that it could not have been planned by the Nazis. But what? . . .

"I think—," Bartlett started to say, hesitating to tell them but knowing that they desperately needed to be warned, "I think the SS has been ordered to pump Zyklon-B down on us as soon as the holes can be drilled."

A moment of stunned silence was broken with gasps of panic.

"We cannot escape then!" Scheinfeld exclaimed. "We have no hope, no—"

Cutting himself off, he listened as the drilling became louder, nearer.

"I thought you said the Heydrich widow wanted *you* alive," Scheinfeld reminded Bartlett. "Why is she causing *this?*"

"For a very good reason," Bartlett replied. "She assumes that I won't allow the deaths of so many other men. She is sure that I will climb out of the tunnel and give myself up if your safety is guaranteed."

Scheinfeld looked back down the line of men in the tunnel, seeing only those nearest him but knowing the others by name.

"I, for one, vote *not* to give the mad widow of one of Satan's worst henchmen the satisfaction she craves," he shouted. "We have fought together in the past, and now, if that is to be our fate, we die *together!* This deranged witch surely could never be trusted to hold to her word anyway. Are you all with me?"

The men shouted agreement. None protested.

Scheinfeld turned to the American.

"Stephen, you do not have to be concerned with any of us leaving your side," he said, smiling reassuringly.

As Bartlett thanked Scheinfeld, he realized that he should not hesitate for a single moment, that he had an obligation to do for the partisans what they had just pledged themselves to do for him.

Yet the other stark truth he faced was that his wife and his son remained somewhere within the confines of Dachau, probably at the medical center.

He remembered what Kellar had told him about the experiments being inflicted upon prisoners, such as injecting them with deadly malaria germs or submerging untold numbers of them, naked, in large tanks filled with near-freezing water.

Stephen Bartlett had come to rescue his loved ones from a woman driven to vengeance by grief. Could he sacrifice himself alongside these valiant partisans and *ignore* what had brought him to that spot in the first place? And yet . . .

Bits and pieces of rock and soil started to drop from the ceiling.

"They have a large opening where the floor collapsed," Scheinfeld spoke in a whisper. "Why these new, much smaller ones?"

"I suspect this gambit is designed to force us toward the troopers," Bartlett replied. "They figure we *must* go where there is fresh air."

He rubbed his chin, praying silently for wisdom, aware that he had no more than seconds left to decide what they should do.

"We stay, we die," Bartlett declared. "But I don't think we should let their kind off so easily. We must make them pay a price for what they are doing to us and to the thousands of men, women, and children imprisoned above us. We might as well try to take some Nazis with us even as we go down ourselves."

"Storm the opening? Are you suggesting that, Stephen?"

Scheinfeld's face showed that he was both excited and alarmed by the prospect of facing a barrage of enemy firepower.

"I am," Bartlett said. "But that mustn't be the only aspect of what we do. It is one thing to die for a cause and quite another to *throw* our lives away."

"If only we could find some way of helping at least a few of the prisoners, since that is why we started this mission in the first place," Scheinfeld reminded him. "And if by helping these poor souls, we could do the same for your wife and your son, would that not be wonderful, my friend?"

The American studied this little man, someone he had not known as recently as a few days earlier yet the two of them might soon die side by side as SS troopers serving the Third Reich cut them down.

He held himself straight, raising his pistol above his head.

"We go together," he declared, "you and I and our comrades here. We fight, prepared to die, if necessary, before our enemies!"

The group of partisans cheered.

"We'll have to work fast," Bartlett cautioned. "I doubt that they'll wait much longer before starting to pump Zyklon-B."

"We have forgotten one thing, Stephen."

"What is that?"

"Getting down on our knees and raising our voices to Jehovah," Scheinfeld said knowingly. "Can a Christian bring himself to do that with a bunch of grizzled old Jews?"

The flow of hydrocyanic acid gas would commence less than half an hour later.

Just before that, the partisans had gathered a short distance beyond the edge of the gaping hole on the cellar floor.

Stephen Bartlett took a quick survey of the conditions directly above. He saw a group of uniformed SS troopers through the now glassless window frames and the open doorway leading out into the main part of Dachau. Lina Heydrich was standing next to a tall man in his late twenties whose appearance seemed rather dashing, her hand holding on to his arm.

Mengele! So young and yet—!

The image Bartlett saw of Josef Mengele, the death doctor of Auschwitz, belied how the man conducted himself. He was a chilling killer, like a relentless machine without heart and soul and human warmth. When he smiled, it was more the smile of a wax dummy gone mad.

"Herman, the tunnel goes on beyond this spot, correct?" Bartlett asked.

"It does, according to the map that Kellar provided," Scheinfeld replied. "But can we trust *anything* from him or Dobrik? It is possible that all of us have been deceived about this from the very start."

"It could be that if Kellar has betrayed us he assumed we would never get beyond this spot. So he'd have no reason to lie about the rest."

Scheinfeld's eyes widened.

"You may be right!" he declared. "What should we do?"

"They'll expect us in fact *not* to trust the rest of the map. They'll assume we're going to try blocking the holes through which the gas will be coming, and failing that, stage a suicide attack, since we'll have no other options."

Scheinfeld studied the American's expression.

"Are you suggesting otherwise, Stephen?" he added.

"Unfortunately we need to fake just what I've indicated. Some of the men will have to do what the Nazis *assume* we will do, and they'll undoubtedly not come out of it alive. If they think *all* of us are acting accordingly, then the element of surprise when we attack from another end of the camp will be maintained."

"The sacrifice of a few good men for the many," Scheinfeld spoke. "How very Christian, Stephen."

"You may be right but it's hardly unknown among the Jewish people, my friend. Consider what happened in A.D. 73 at Masada."

"But remember the aftermath! Two thousand years of what we call the *Diaspora* passed before we could ever return to our homeland. What good did it do? What victory was achieved? Show me anything but defeat!"

Bartlett placed his hands on Scheinfeld's shoulders.

"You *do* know the answer, Herman," he said with great patience. "Masada came to be a symbol for every Jew."

Scheinfeld nodded wearily as he bowed his head, his hands folded in front of him.

"Eleazar ben Ya'ir, the zealots' leader, said death in rebellion against their oppressors was far more preferable than surviving for another day the humiliating loss of liberty Israel had been suffering as a nation," he conceded. "That remarkable man and his followers instilled in every Jew worth the name a collective obsession that has carried us through to . . . this very moment."

When he glanced up at the American, his eyes were wet.

"We will carry out this plan as you say," he pledged, "for you have spoken well, Stephen Bartlett. You have become our latest Eleazar ben Ya'ir, though I suspect you will not wear that mantle comfortably."

Scheinfeld smiled as he added, "We *are* prepared, I believe, to do for you what ben Ya'ir's men did for him so long ago."

At that comment, Bartlett found it difficult to rein in his emotions, though he recognized that he must seem in control of himself to maintain the confidence of these valiant men.

"Praise God for that!" he told Scheinfeld. "Now here is what I think should happen: If the decoy plan is successful, the rest of us will have gotten to where Kellar said the relatively healthy prisoners are kept, the ones strong enough to be able to endure, for a time, the rigors of a work detail, which is their only value to the tyrants running Dachau.

"I have no reason to doubt the truthfulness of such information. It would seem, according to Aryan dogma, quite consistent and reasonable that these particular prisoners be separated from the sick and infirm. As far as the Nazis are concerned, the others are just about worthless except perhaps for experiments at the medical building where mindless devils can use them as guinea pigs.

"We'll arm the whole group, Herman, using whatever extra weapons and ammunition we've managed to bring along, and then we'll come at the SS troopers from another direction, catching them off-guard, since their attention will be focused on the *Leichenkeller*."

"They would *never* suspect this from us!" Scheinfeld exclaimed, his expression brightening at the implications.

"We must pray that is the case," Bartlett muttered. "If not, then the only ambush victims could become us."

16

The Zyklon-B was ready.

A dark gray rubber hose connected to a tank truck—once used to carry gasoline but now modified for genocidal use, its shipment of poisonous gas provided by I. G. Farben, Germany's leading manufacturer of chemicals—had been stuck into one of the holes leading directly into the tunnel below.

"The others have been dug strictly for decoy purposes," Richard Gluecks explained proudly as Lina Heydrich stood beside him in the middle of the concrete street that stretched from one end of Dachau to the other. "They may try to plug each of the holes, thinking they can prevent the gas from reaching them. What they are not aware of is that only one of these holes will be used. They cannot possibly close off each one. We have opened up far too many. But any effort they extend will be distracting, tiring."

Gluecks smiled coolly.

"The dummy holes are quite visible," he said. "The only one we will use is not in the ceiling of the tunnel at all. It happens to be much lower, in fact, quite near the floor. It was put there before the Jews ever arrived."

"I can see that took some careful planning, Richard," the widow spoke admiringly, "and, I might add, some skill."

"We have known about all this for the better part of the night. You see, we had a very good man inform us."

"Who was that, Richard?"

He took her hand in his own.

"You speak with some passion," he said, "even with so few words."

He kissed the back of that hand.

"Gustav Dobrik was the one, ostensibly a partisan prisoner. After some little time had passed, he pretended, with astonishing conviction, to be somewhat sympathetic to the American and the others. Just after midnight, he and his men managed to overpower the partisans who had been left behind. It was an easy task, I might say, skilled professionals against homespun amateurs, Jews at that!"

From the start, Lina knew that charming Gluecks into doing her bidding would not be a difficult task. The two of them were lovers during the months prior to her courtship by Reinhard Heydrich and had maintained discreet but always chaste contact ever since then.

Frau Heydrich had been instrumental in getting Gluecks promoted from being assistant to the commandant of Dachau when it initially opened early in 1933 to assuming the leadership of the sprawling network of some fifty other camps in Germany seven years later. She hadn't had to work very hard at achieving that promotion since Gluecks was already held in high regard by Paul Josef Goebbels who admired Gluecks's part in running Dachau as the tightest and most efficient in the entire camp system.

Days gone forever, she thought as images of her husband danced across her mind; she reluctantly returned from past glories to cope with the demands of the present.

Searchlights played across Dachau, lighting every corner of it.

Gluecks pointed to these as he said, "As soon as the Jews come storming out of the entrance to the *Leichenkeller,* the lights will be turned off. They will have no idea what is happening and will be tempted to retreat, but because of the gas behind them, they will realize instantly that this is impossible. Each of our marksmen is armed with a rifle equipped with an experimental sight that will be able to pinpoint every single one of them, Lina."

"What is experimental about that?" she asked.

"It can see in the dark! Is that not astonishing? The Allies seem to be decades behind us in this."

"So you can pick them off one by one?"

"Forty marksmen for forty-odd partisans!"

"Except one, I trust."

"The American, of course."

"How will they recognize him?"

"Each one has a photograph."

Lina threw her head back and roared with laughter.

"You are amazing!" she exclaimed.

"You told me much the same thing that very first night we spent together outside Munich, Frau Heydrich. Do you remember?"

She nodded with some enthusiasm.

"It was true then; it is nonetheless so now."

Lina was becoming tired of waiting.

"This is *so* boring, Richard," she said.

"Shall we start then?" Gluecks inquired.

"If you will, please."

He turned to the men at the trunk.

"Let it begin," he said as he waved his arm about in an extravagant gesture before returning his attention to Lina Heydrich. "Shall we sit back, my dear?"

"Have you some French wine? Burgundy perhaps?"

He snapped his fingers.

A prison inmate hurried out of the shadows.

The widow froze, sucking in her breath at the sight of him.

Gluecks noticed this.

"Does he offend you?" he asked, alarmed.

The inmate stood before the two of them, most of his teeth gone except for some protruding roots turned dark with decay, his gums so red they seemed to be covered in bloody sores. His clothes, however, were in better shape than those worn by his fellow prisoners but, still, he looked to be what he was, a human being who had suffered bestial treatment.

Frau Heydrich turned her head away as casually as possible and muttered, "It is nothing." She paused, then quickly added, lying as she did so, "I was thinking how much like an old Gustav Dore woodcut he seems, like a misshapen creature out of Hades. No wonder I hear stories of some of your most hardened *Schutzstaffel* troopers having nightmares after spending a few weeks with his kind."

"So he *has* upset you!" Gluecks pressed.

"It *would* be better if someone else served us that wine," she admitted emotionlessly. "Will you see to it, Dickie, my dear?"

"At once," he replied, jumping to his feet and grabbing the inmate by the neck, then dragging him out of sight.

The widow of the Butcher of Prague looked at her hands and wondered why, suddenly, they had begun to tremble.

Agonized cries . . .

Men were crying in pain behind them.

"The gas!" Scheinfeld screamed, interrupting the digging as he did so. "They're dying now. We cannot do this, Stephen. We *have* to help them."

Bartlett grabbed his shoulder.

"We knew this would happen," he said. "There is no other way."

"They are going to be bleeding from their mouths and noses. Their bowels are—"

"Listen, please, listen to me! By the time we would reach them, it *will* be over . . . nothing left but their lifeless bodies. We can only help the poor souls above us right now. Isn't that the point, Herman? If not, we might as well die with the others and not accomplish anything that is just and noble this night."

Scheinfeld was about to say something in response when the sound of gunshots joined the shouts of the dying.

"We have so little time if we are to surprise the Nazis at all," Bartlett pleaded. "Don't you see that?"

The other man nodded reluctantly.

"If you were Jewish, you would understand," he muttered.

"I am a Christian, remember," Bartlett retorted, with a touch of anger. "Two thousand years ago, countless numbers of us were being thrown to the lions while thousands issued bloodthirsty cheers!"

The digging continued, seconds passing as the sounds of confrontation continued.

Finally—

"The floor!" someone yelled. "I've got through to the floor!"

Less than a minute later, they had broken into a hut-like building where prisoners were sitting up, startled by the sounds below the floor and then by the men who streamed through a gaping hole in the middle of it.

"God in Heaven!" one of the partisans reacted in shock to the sight of several scores of bony-framed men crowded into rabbit-hutch sleeping arrangements, their unwashed, thinly clothed bodies sending up a heavy stench into the chill air that reached through the thin wood of that dilapidated structure.

Scheinfeld told everyone what was happening.

All were eager to help out.

Those who seemed the strongest and mentally the most coherent were given pistols and rifles as well as ammunition and as many grenades as they could handle.

One of the younger prisoners, though he appeared to be many

years older from the ordeal he had suffered daily at Dachau, shuffled up to Bartlett.

"American flyers," he mumbled.

"Here?" Bartlett asked, incredulous, suspecting that the Allies were unaware that any of the extermination or concentration camps were doubling as POW enclaves.

Americans being shoved into ovens, he thought, *or starving to death or being shot in the back of the head!*

He clenched his fists, the knuckles turning white, pain shooting up through the fingers.

"In the medical center," the young man's voice intruded, "along with a very pretty American woman and her little boy."

Bartlett felt perspiration abruptly cover his body.

"My wife, my son," he said, barely able to say the words.

"Sir?" this young man asked pitiably.

"Yes, my brother," Bartlett asked.

The other hesitated, as though not understanding.

"You call me brother," he repeated, a bewildered expression on his long, thin face. "I have not heard that word for a very long time now."

"How many years have you been here?"

"Five . . ."

Now it was the American's turn to look uncomprehending.

"They cannot seem to kill me," the young man told him. "I have been strong. They are amazed, these foul beasts. I came here almost as a child . . ."

Someone else spoke up.

"He talks to us about God, this one. Every day, he repeats Bible verses he has memorized. He gives us hope, even from the New Testament. As more and more of us have been dying over the past awful months, sometimes in his arms, our great friend here talks with great joy of angels coming to take us home to our blessed heavenly Father. We love this man. Only God could give him such extraordinary strength."

"What is your name?" Bartlett asked.

"Abraham Holtzman."

"Take these."

Bartlett handed him a machine gun and two grenades.

"From talking of heaven," Holtzman spoke ironically as he held them, "to sending those devils straight to hell . . ."

"Can you do this?" Bartlett asked.

"Is the pope Catholic?"

17

In a short while it will be dawn," Heinrich Himmler spoke wistfully. "Fifteen years ago, not such a long time as far as the verdicts of history go I think you will agree, I was raising chickens. I would be awake at dawn each day, looking out at the sun rising above the trees that surrounded our farm. My hands were dirty by late afternoon but I could wash them off easily enough then."

He sighed, not comfortable revealing himself even to the Desert Fox but somehow driven to do so anyway . . . better before such a man than the sniveling bootlicks who usually hovered around him, ready to agree with everything he said or did but not so trustworthy that they wouldn't betray him to Martin Bormann perhaps, a rival who was increasingly uncomfortable with the power base that Himmler had been building for nearly a decade.

"And now you have men, women, and children living in worse conditions than your poultry ever did!" Erwin Rommel exclaimed.

As they sat in the back seat of the special Mercedes, with its armor-plated siding and bulletproof windows, Himmler seemed momentarily in a more sympathetic frame of mind than Rommel had thought would be the case.

"You cannot, I have heard, stand the sight of human blood, Heinrich," he pressed dangerously.

Rommel expected an immediate, indignant, perhaps violent reaction.

"And what is your feeling about that rumor, Erwin?" Himmler replied coolly.

"I have come to believe there is some truth in this. At every camp you have visited, you have become ill and ultimately had to excuse yourself. Is this traceable only to your lifelong history of severe headaches, stomach colic, and other ailments; does one or more of these ailments just happen to strike each time?"

Himmler took off his pince-nez glasses and rubbed his gray-blue eyes.

"You have not mentioned Konrad Morgan," he spoke softly.

Rommel knew about this obscure but dedicated man, yet he wanted Himmler to introduce Morgan into the conversation.

"The assistant *Schutzstaffel* judge? Yes, I was planning on bringing him up if there were time before we arrived at Dachau."

"He seems to have gone beyond his original duties . . ."

"Which were strictly to ferret out SS corruption at the camps but recently has included investigating stories of brutality directed against the inmates."

"Strange for a man who is known in some quarters as a monster, is it not?" Himmler emphasized.

"Could it be, as the Americans would say, that some chickens are coming home to roost, Heinrich?"

Himmler said nothing.

"What about Karl Koch?" Rommel asked abruptly. "Are your actions in that case the work of a conscienceless monster?"

For a moment he thought he saw Himmler's right cheek twitch.

"You ordered Koch's arrest. Why?" Rommel continued.

"Because, at Buchenwald, commandant Koch embezzled more than a hundred thousand marks of the Third Reich's money."

"More than that, Heinrich, more than that."

Himmler seemed uncustomarily hesitant.

"The *murders,* that was the real reason why you went after him. An *SS-Gericht* conducted an investigation and found him guilty. You could not tolerate the bestial behavior perpetrated by this loathsome one and his . . ."

Rommel deliberately hesitated, gauging Himmler's reaction to what he obviously was going to say next, about the wife of Karl Koch, and giving himself a chance to interpolate something.

"That woman, yes," the words came, as Rommel had suspected, as though spoken in slow motion.

"She was called the Bitch of Buchenwald, by prisoners and guards alike, Heinrich. The court described Ilse Koch as a demon. She was the one who started the most grotesque fad known to mankind."

Himmler's right hand shot up, indicating a demand for silence.

"She ordered lampshades, book covers, and gloves to be made of skin taken from *living* prisoners, Heinrich. It had to be supple. It could not be hardened by death. They screamed pitiably as it was torn off their bodies. Sometimes she would do the deed herself, and, it is said, achieve a degree of sexual satisfaction from their anguish."

"Enough!" Himmler blurted out then. "You are the finest general in the modern history of our beloved *Deustchland,* which we both serve with great valor and earnestness, but, Erwin, you do assume an invincibility on your behalf that may be your undoing instead!"

Still Rommel would not be stopped.

"Is it my death you are implying?" he asked pointedly. "I have been close to death often on the battlefield. I have seen it snatch away thousands of my countrymen. It is so simple, Heinrich, you know, this matter of dying."

Rommel pulled out his Luger and placed the nozzle under his chin.

"If you but ask, I shall end even now this misery that life truly has become of late," he declared. "You can tell the German people that a partisan bullet was responsible."

In a sudden motion, Himmler reached over and grabbed the weapon, wrenching it from the Desert Fox's hand.

For a split second he seemed about to aim it at his own head. Then he placed it on his open palm.

"Neither of us is so much a coward," he said.

Rommel took the gun and returned it to its holster at his side.

"Nor so much a madman that we can witness the horror of the camps and avoid nights that scream our guilt at us from the darkness."

18

One by one, the partisans who remained behind to act as decoys were killed as they emerged from the tunnel. They had little chance to retreat. Nazi marksmen encountered no trouble zeroing in on them with their experimental infrared telescopic sights.

From his vantage point at the other end of Dachau, Herman Scheinfeld glimpsed a dozen brave men with whom he had become close over the months as they dropped almost immediately to the ground, their faces contorted, blood spurting from wounds in their chests, their necks, their foreheads. Most kept on shooting as long as they could. Two of the men saw where several of the marksmen were grouped, on a guard tower near the main entrance to the camp. They managed to throw grenades in that direction, splintering the tower's foundation and toppling it before both partisans were cut down.

"It is a slaughter ground!" Scheinfeld exclaimed, turning away briefly. "We must act soon, Stephen."

"This building is on the east side of the camp," Bartlett said. "There is another right beside us but we can't spare the firepower, too much duplication, so the rest of our men should arm the prisoners on the west side."

"I will go with them," Scheinfeld agreed. "You stay here. In fifteen minutes you attack; then we follow two minutes later, right?"

The American nodded as he said, "Troopers will be sent into the tunnel to make sure no one is left behind. As soon as they enter, they will be hit by the second group of men."

Bartlett turned to those men.

"Most of the gas should be dissipated by then," he said. "It has no real staying power. That's why the troopers will see no need to wear masks. Hit them in the head if you can. They've been trained to keep shooting as long as they can, no matter how badly hurt they are. They don't need to think about this. It's become instinctive by now, machine-like perhaps.

"You could get them in the legs and I imagine they *would* fall, but they'd still have their weapons clutched in their hands. That's why hitting them in the forehead or between the eyes is critical. One shot should do it. Then hurry back here. We need everyone here and ready without further delay."

Bartlett prayed the plan would work, that Richard Gluecks would be blind with rage, embarrassed by a ragtag bunch of simple Jews and driven to roar out orders for a fresh contingent of troopers to storm the tunnel, more heavily armed this time, possibly with flamethrowers in addition to guns. The commandant of Dachau would see to it that all attention and manpower was focused on that one area at the northern end of the camp.

And then we hit them from behind! Bartlett thought. *The bulk of their forces will be deployed by then, either in the open, waiting, or in the tunnel itself, not realizing the clever game we are playing with them.*

He glanced at his watch.

Anyone still in the tunnel minutes from now will be blown apart by the explosives I planted near the entrance and farther back, or buried by collapsing dirt and rock, he thought. *If, that is, there are no more foul-ups in our planning. At that precise moment we attack from the exact opposite corners of this camp!*

He turned and looked at the prisoners standing side by side with the Jewish partisans, the crowded conditions even worse now that more than twenty additional men had been packed inside.

Abraham Holtzman saw the expression on his face.

"We *are* ready!" he declared proudly. "When your men first burst outside, we will cover you, shooting down any black-shirts we see."

"The woman, too, if any of us spot her," a faint voice came from among the tired, hungry men in that building.

Bartlett flinched at that. As much of a symbol of unleashed hatred, vengeance, Nazi inhumanity and genocide as Lina Heydrich had become, he still resisted shooting an unarmed woman. He couldn't help thinking of her children, so steeped in the corrupt philosophy of the Third Reich and yet still young enough to be deprogrammed, to be made more than mindless puppets of rampant fascism.

Could I actually pull the trigger if she were standing before me? Bartlett asked himself. *Would I be able to blow to pieces—?*

He knew the answer depended in part on what had happened to his wife and his son. Could they be in unimaginable pain as they were strapped to surgical tables, their insides cut open? Or dying in a tank of near-freezing water?

Or—

Mengele's repertoire of experiments reportedly wasn't limited to those two instances of barbarism. Was it something else he had inflicted upon them?

Bartlett caught another glimpse of Lina Heydrich. She was leaning over, nibbling at Richard Gluecks's ear and laughing heartily.

He raised a rifle, found her in its sights.

Dachau was less than half a mile ahead of them.

Himmler always traveled with a heavily armed fleet of trucks in front and back of his vehicle. He had never been as lax about security as Reinhard Heydrich, but the other man's assassination had raised a red flag for all the top Nazis as well as some of the lesser ones, and substantial manpower and weapons were transferred to safeguard top brass who had more reason than ever to fear sudden attack.

The sound of rifle and machine-gun fire reached the caravan, followed by a series of explosions.

Himmler bolted straight up in his seat.

"Is there some connection," he demanded coldly, "between what we are hearing ahead of us and why we happen to be arriving here at this very moment?"

"I have no idea," Rommel replied. "My men would never participate in an attack against German property, so I fail to see . . ."

More explosions.

Their Mercedes lurched to one side, then stopped abruptly.

Rommel was thrown against Himmler, their driver tossed forward as the steering wheel snapped and his head collided with the bulletproof glass, crushing in his forehead, fragments ricocheting through his brain and killing him instantly.

Shouting.

Rommel tried to steady himself, pushing away from Himmler, who seemed dazed for a moment but otherwise was unhurt.

The car had come to rest at a sharp, nearly vertical angle.

Rommel raised himself slightly from his seat, and saw something astonishing . . . the group of four trucks that accompanied them, two in front, two in the back, were also stopped simultaneously *by the ground collapsing from under them!*

SS troopers were clambering out, some limping, others shaking their heads as they tried to get their bearings.

Rommel managed to climb over the edge of the Mercedes. He stumbled toward the men who had gathered to one side.

"We could be attacked any moment," he said. "Do not wait for orders from me to fire. Do so at the first indication of movement."

He turned toward the Mercedes. Himmler was still dazed as he weakly tried to get out of the back seat.

"Help him," Rommel said calmly.

Two troopers hurried to the car and carefully lifted Himmler over the side, which was tilted upward.

Within seconds, Himmler seemed coherent and stable again.

"The ground just gave way," he said. "Those explosions must have weakened it."

"Tunnels . . . ," Rommel told him. "I wonder if there are tunnels weaving *throughout* this entire region."

"Under Dachau?"

"And who knows where else? How many of our military installations? Our factories? Even Berlin itself?"

Himmler lost whatever color his pale features normally held.

"Sir!" a trooper shouted as he came up to them, still holding a pair of binoculars. "I reconnoitered the situation ahead. From what I can see, there is a rebellion of some sort in progress. Our men are being killed by armed prisoners and others I cannot identify but who obviously are not from the camp!"

Rommel waited rather awkwardly for a moment since he understood that Himmler was not a military tactician, yet the other man was also his superior, and he, the lesser officer, could not appear to be taking over.

Fortunately, Himmler himself comprehended this and deferred to Rommel with a simple nod, tacitly acknowledging his greater experience on the battlefield.

"They could not be expecting us," the Desert Fox told them. "Anything we do will take them by surprise."

He had fifty men at his disposal but no knowledge of the size of the enemy.

"The prisoners have been treated harshly for a long time and will not be a serious problem," he said, careful not to glance at Himmler for emphasis. "They are too weak to offer much resistance.

Yet some may have weapons of one sort or another, if only knives, so we must not disregard them altogether."

He stared at the troopers.

"It is the ones involved with them that we must consider the overriding threat," he went on. "They are probably partisans and—"

Rommel saw the expressions of contempt on the faces of most of the troopers gathered in front of him.

"Do *not* view these men in that manner!" he demanded. "A shot that strikes the heart or the brain of any one of us is fatal, whether it is fired by an inexperienced Jew or a decorated soldier with years of experience. Any complacency on our part in battle becomes our enemy's weapon, and we must never hand it to them so blithely!"

He went on to tell the men that they would have to strike the camp from all four sides, roughly a dozen of them each to the north, south, east, and west.

"Our numbers are limited," he acknowledged, "but we must give the impression of a much greater force."

One of the troopers raised his hand.

"What about the inmates?" he asked. "Some will have weapons, some may not. What are our guidelines about shooting them?"

Rommel was about to address that issue when Himmler spoke up instead.

"Shoot anyone who is not in uniform!" he told them.

Rommel froze at the searing image of already ravaged men, women, and children, armed or otherwise, dying by the hundreds as bullets tore into their bodies. Even on the battlefield, he had made it a personal mission to see that Allied *soldiers* were not harmed after they were captured, but now *civilian* prisoners were going to be in great danger, helpless bystanders caught in crossfire.

"Sir, may I speak with you for a moment?" Rommel asked, hoping he had concealed any tension in his voice.

He and Himmler walked several feet away from the troopers.

"Is it wise to force the murder of so many of the innocents?" Rommel questioned as soon as they were out of hearing range.

"What is the alternative?" Himmler demanded.

"For the men to be as selective as possible rather than simply opening up and firing indiscriminately."

"But being selective, as you say, requires time, if only seconds, which would give the enemy the advantage in such instances, would you not agree, Field Marshal Rommel? It is better that they simply—"

Rommel interrupted Himmler, something he would not have dared under other circumstances.

"What if the American and his family are killed?" he asked.

"What if they are *involved*," the other man replied.

Rommel knew the dangerous ground he was treading.

"Then we must face the fact that our vengeful female adversary will have had her victory. Are you willing to tolerate her gloating?"

He had hit a nerve in Himmler.

Unlike Hitler, who seemed inclined to act in a relatively chivalrous manner even toward rather brash German *frauleins* of his acquaintance, Himmler became offended when someone like Lina Heydrich refused to obey him.

"We must immediately communicate our intentions to the men, Heinrich," Rommel said pointedly. "What shall we tell them?"

"We tell them to be as selective as possible," Himmler replied. "Avoid unarmed civilians but only if it is not life-threatening to the troopers to do so. Should the American and his family be found, they are to be protected at all costs."

"And the still-grieving widow? What do we tell the troops about her?"

Heinrich Himmler looked at Rommel, the barest hint of a smile on his pale, schoolteacher-like face.

"We must all hope she does not catch a stray bullet," he said. "What a tragedy that would be for the Fatherland!"

19

*T*roopers will be sent into the tunnel to make sure no one is left behind. As soon as they enter, they will be hit by the second group of men. Most of the gas should be dissipated by then. It has no real staying power. That's why the troopers will see no need to wear masks. Hit them in the head if you can. They've been trained to keep shooting as long as they can, no matter how badly hurt they are. They don't need to think about this. It's become instinctive by now, machine-like perhaps.

Richard Gluecks would be blind with rage, embarrassed by a rag-tag bunch of simple Jews and driven to roar out orders for a fresh contingent of troopers to storm the tunnel, more heavily armed this time, possibly with flamethrowers in addition to guns. The commandant of Dachau would see to it that all attention and manpower was focused on that one area at the northern end of the camp.

It happened as Stephen Bartlett had planned.

And while the troopers were involved in raiding the tunnel, a contingent of partisans and prisoners opened fire from two locations at the southern and western corners of Dachau.

In the meantime, the American and the rest of the partisans had fanned out along opposite sides of the camp, moving up the perimeter to get closer to the troopers who remained out in the open while their comrades went below.

"*Now!*" Bartlett commanded.

Herman Scheinfeld, acting as Bartlett's surrogate on the other side, issued the same order, the two groups moving in unison.

Grenades showered through the air like hailstones.

Bartlett, resisting temptation, told the men to try and avoid hitting Gluecks and Lina Heydrich. Mengele had been seen retreating to the medical center.

Explosions caused by the grenades now sealed the tunnel entrance tight, trapping a large number of SS troopers underground. The relatively small force left in the open was decimated by the unexpected attack.

Gluecks and the widow were grabbed by partisans and held to one side.

After watching the action from their cramped quarters, thousands of prisoners cheered, convinced now that they would gain freedom.

Bartlett, Scheinfeld, and the other men emerged in the center of Dachau, standing on the concrete pavement that stretched nearly from one end to the other.

Lina Heydrich was dragged over to stand in front of him.

"It is not ended!" she declared, though the stridency of her voice had become strangely less than convincing, giving her the manner of someone who was protesting just a bit too much. "There is much more between us not settled by what has happened this day."

Scheinfeld spoke then, his voice filled with contempt, "You risk so much for the memory of a monster!"

"He was *not* a monster!" she retorted. "The legacy he wanted was only that of a pure Europe, a pure world not tainted by the corruption of disease-laden Jew blood."

One by one, prisoners were streaming outside, some able to make it only as they were supported by others. Many of the children walked alone, their parents long since buried in ditches or burned to ashes or planted in large fields to fertilize rolling expanses of multicolored, sweet-scented flowers.

A crowd soon gathered around the two men and this woman.

"You speak of a legacy," Bartlett said. "Here it is. Look at them! Do not allow what you see *ever* to pass from your mind."

She clenched her left hand into a fist and raised it in front of the American's face.

"I shall not stop until you are—" She stopped.

Something was tugging at her other hand.

A scarcely audible voice called to her, "Momma! Momma!"

Lina Heydrich glanced down at her side.

A little girl had been smiling as she looked upward to Lina, then that smile was gone as the child backed away, eyes suddenly filling with tears.

"You probably resembled her mother," Bartlett remarked.

"Look at her, how thin she is. See the dirt all over her body, the bruises. The guards rape little children here, and in other camps, you know."

Lina clamped her palms to her ears, trying to block out his words.

Bartlett grabbed her wrists and pried her hands away.

"Pandora's box is open," he said. "You cannot close it so easily. Nor can you pretend it doesn't exist or that the blame rests anywhere but at your husband's feet."

He swung her around and dragged her up to the crowd, forcing her to face other children who stood in front of the group.

"*All* of them are alone now!" he went on. "How it would be for *your* children if *they* saw you shoved into one of the gas chambers and were made to watch as your body lost its ability to control your bodily function and you slipped and fell into a pile of your own wastes or perhaps those from the woman next to you?"

"No more!" she begged. "*In God's name,* no more!"

"How often are *Jewish* prisoners given mercy when *they* call out for it?" Bartlett demanded. "Or are they taken instead to the medical building where psychopaths, clothed in the specious respectability of a doctor's calling, cut up human flesh and laugh as their victims cough up their agony in gushers of blood?"

She screamed in pain but he refused to let go as he dragged her toward the gray-toned building where he prayed he would find his wife, his son. Herman Scheinfeld and several partisans followed.

Bartlett kicked open the door and pulled Lina Heydrich with him.

She stopped struggling as she saw what was inside.

In the center of the twenty-by-thirty-foot main room, doors on either side leading to smaller ones, were three surgical tables with various trays on top of them. Some of the instruments had not been cleaned and still contained the grisly residue of whatever experiments had been done that day. In bottles on shelves hanging from another wall were bits and pieces of—

The widow of the Butcher of Prague quickly turned away, unable to look at the contents any longer, and saw, on the other side of the room, that Natalie Bartlett and son Andrew were hanging by their feet from ropes attached to a metal rod protruding from the ceiling. Their faces red and bloated from lack of circulation, their eyes bulged wide as they saw their beloved husband and father suddenly enter the room. Andrew still wore his flannel pajama top over much-too-big trousers held to his waist with a belt; around his rope-bound ankles the cuffs had been rolled into big coils that now fell heavily almost to his knees as he was suspended upside down from the ceiling. Natalie wore thin white cotton prison pajamas. As she hung, inverted, from the metal bar, the loose top fell downward to pool under armpits, but the bottoms, enormously big on her slim legs, drooped over her chest, nearly reaching her chin. The blood-tinged bandage over her chest wound was visible through the pajama fabric.

When he saw his father, Andrew twisted and struggled, reaching for Bartlett and causing the rope to swing him dangerously close to the wall. But Natalie, weakened from her wound, was only able to moan. Their mouths were taped shut. Mengele stood by, tightly holding the leashes of two snarling German shepherds with his left hand, a Luger in the other.

"They are *quite* fast, I assure you!" Mengele declared. "And these two have very strong jaws. It would be some time before you could pry them off."

Stephen Bartlett did not move, his gaze going from the dogs to Natalie and Andrew and back again.

Scheinfeld pushed into the building from behind the American.

"We do whatever you tell us, Stephen," he said. "I personally would like to—"

"Quiet, Jew!" Mengele sneered. "What is at issue here is not my fate but what happens to this sweet little boy and his mother, would you not agree, Jew-lover?"

Bartlett said nothing.

"I want safe passage out of this camp," Mengele demanded. "I shall take both of them along to ensure that you do not try to trick me."

"If we refuse and you turn the dogs loose, you'll die. You are hardly bargaining with the right chips; surely you know that," Bartlett remarked.

"True, yet only up to a point," Mengele said. "But then, after it is all over, what will be left of your loved ones?"

He smiled crookedly as he added, "It seems that I *do* control this situation after all, does it not?"

Wrong.

Scheinfeld sprang toward the dogs. They pulled loose and were on him in an instant. Mengele swung the Luger toward Bartlett and, firing erratically, caught him in the lower arm. Bartlett stumbled, then fell.

Mengele laughed as he aimed his pistol again at Bartlett, whose own gun had fallen to one side.

"*No!*" Lina Heydrich yelled. "This must stop!"

" *This,* as you call it, is happening only because of you, Frau Heydrich," Mengele reminded her.

"Then I have the right to stop it!" she declared as she walked slowly toward him, her hand out, palm up. "Give me the Luger, Josef."

"I give you *only* the back of my hand, woman!" Mengele growled as he hit her across the chin and she was flung against a long white lab table, causing it to collapse in a shower of broken test tubes and jars.

He strode over to Bartlett, who was struggling to get to his feet.

Mengele kicked him in the face and sent him sprawling back to the floor.

Outside there was the sound of gunfire.

"I wondered why no one was rushing in to rescue you," Mengele spoke. "Your fellow conspirators must have their hands full now. It seems that that pathetic little band of Jews may be *trapped* inside a camp they undoubtedly hoped to *liberate*. Is that not a rather delightful irony to contemplate before *you* die?"

He stood in front of Bartlett, who was holding his arm tightly, trying to stop the bleeding. He aimed the Luger, his finger closing around the trigger and starting to press on it.

Suddenly his face contorted, eyes widening in pain. He spun around and saw Lina Heydrich as he realized she had grabbed a scalpel and plunged it into his back. Before he could shoot her, she used it again, this time slashing the well-honed blade into his gun hand.

Mengele lurched forward, grabbing her around the neck. She managed to cut him again near his Adam's apple, but not deeply, before he forced her to the floor and her grip loosened on the scalpel.

"*The dogs!*" Bartlett screamed.

The German shepherds had finished with Herman Scheinfeld's body and were attracted by the confusion at the other end of that large room. Gathering their back feet together, the dogs got ready to spring.

With his wounded arm held against his body, Bartlett used his other hand to retrieve the Luger that had fallen out of Mengele's hand; he shot one of the dogs in the chest. The dog hit the floor, jerking spasmodically, then was still.

As he aimed at the other dog, it attacked him.

The German shepherd's full weight fell against him and he was knocked onto his back, the animal's large mouth snapping at his throat.

"Grab the scalpel!" he heard Lina Heydrich shout hoarsely.

She threw it toward him and he caught it by the handle, and, in the next motion, slashed the scalpel up and under the dog's chin, opening its throat. A sound that was a combination of gurgling and a sudden loud whine came from the eighty-pound body just as it fell away from him and onto its side.

The American managed to stand, then hurried over to Natalie and Andrew.

"I'm going to cut the rope," he said, as he held out the scalpel. "Reach out your arms to cushion your fall."

As Bartlett tried to help his family with his one good arm Lina Heydrich approached them, a similar surgical instrument in one hand.

"You take care of your wife," she told him. "Let me cut the boy's rope."

Bartlett nodded, and they both went to work. In less than a minute, Natalie and Andrew were free. The three of them embraced, something they had wondered if they would ever be able to do again.

"My husband never allowed me to visit any of the camps," Lina said. "He told me the awful reports about them were merely Allied propaganda seeping in. He assured me that, while the conditions were certainly basic, it was not true that prisoners were being subjected to such barbaric treatment."

She threw up her hands in front of her.

"What was I to do? Please tell me that. How *could* I believe anyone but Reinhard? I loved him so much, I truly did!"

"You accepted none of it?" Bartlett asked skeptically. "You thought everything that was being revealed about the camps was false?"

She hesitated.

"At first, yes. I . . . I assumed Reinhard was telling me the truth."

"What about later? What about some of the photographs that leaked out?"

"I knew *then* that he had been lying. But . . ."

She had a dazed, scared look in her eyes as she said, "I still could not stop loving him." Then she fell forward, into Bartlett's arms, sobbing.

But the tears lasted only a moment. Lina Heydrich stepped back, her expression now emotionless.

"You must leave immediately," she said.

"But I cannot desert those men!" Bartlett protested.

"To stay is to surrender your loved ones *again* to that kind of monster!" she retorted as she pointed to Mengele, who was moaning as he lay half-conscious in a widening pool of blood on the floor.

The combat outside had intensified, with more screams filling the air amidst the noise of explosions and gunfire.

"You are one man, Stephen; a remarkable man, yes, but from the sound of it, you would be sacrificing everything out there and gaining nothing. You would not change the outcome for *them* but you *would* be throwing away the lives of your wife and your son."

Bartlett could not dispute what she had said.

"Will you go with us?" he asked.

She smiled slightly.

"I am a creature of this nation as it now stands. I shall live with it as we emerge victorious in this war—or I shall go down with it in ruins."

"But why sacrifice yourself when you now know what your precious *Deutschland* is capable of?"

"Camps like Dachau *are* unholy places, yes, but the war itself is as just in its purpose as it ever was. We *had* to be liberated from the tyranny of others."

"And stand proud on the world stage? Can you ever hope to do that now? With the blood of millions draining into the soil of this homeland of yours?"

She shrugged her shoulders.

"I am not your concern. Go now before you have lost this chance to escape."

She reached out and touched his cheek.

"I wish—," she started to say, then turned away.

Andrew grabbed his father's hand, his eyes wide with fear.

"Where will we go?" he asked.

"There are men posted near the camp who . . . ," Stephen Bartlett started to explain, then cast a wary glance at the widow.

She grinned knowingly.

"I will go outside," she said. "You do not have to worry about me."

As she started toward the door, Bartlett called to her, "Don't! Stay here . . . please."

"You can *trust* me then?"

"I don't know if I can. But I have to wonder if you would suddenly throw away those very lives that you've just now helped to save."

She nodded.

"If you and I live through whatever is left of this madness, let me prepare a meal for you and your family if I am able. Reinhard always told me how good I could cook . . ."

The words choked in her throat. She waved them on, out the rear exit.

Stephen Bartlett lingered at the mangled body of Herman Scheinfeld. Astonishingly, the man was still breathing, his eyes open though only a little, his lips moving slowly.

Bartlett bent down beside him.

"Shoot me," Scheinfeld mumbled.

"I cannot, my brother! . . ." the American told him as gently as he could.

"Do not let them get me! They could keep me alive just long enough to tell . . . to tell them—"

Scheinfeld's fingers, trembling, closed around the front of Bartlett's battered brown-leather flight jacket.

"Use your gun," he gasped. "Prevent them . . . from getting me . . . to betray those good men . . . who must survive . . . to carry on our cause."

"You're asking me to murder you," Bartlett objected.

"I'm pleading with you . . . to protect men like me and the others elsewhere in this nation . . . men whose names only Snyder and I knew in their entirety . . . if the Gestapo gets me, I . . . I might crack, Stephen . . . I might be forced to betray my comrades . . . *please don't let the butchers have that chance!"*

Bartlett raised the Luger and in anguish, aimed it at the other man's head, perspiration beading on his own brow.

"Do it, Stephen!" Scheinfeld. *"You must do it!"*

As Bartlett was about to turn aside the weapon, unable to grant what his friend wanted, Scheinfeld, using the last of whatever strength he had left, raised himself up suddenly and jerked the Luger toward him, forcing the American's finger against the trigger. As the gun went off Stephen Bartlett could hear his son, Andrew, scream in shock, horrified by the deadly results of the point-blank shot.

Bartlett spun around and yelled at Natalie, who was holding Andrew in her arms. "Out . . . *now!* We have no time!"

"Stephen, in the next room . . . ," she told him, "*five American pilots are confined there!*"

What Rommel saw was a force of partisans greater by 20 percent than the number of men with Himmler and himself. But he also factored in the element of surprise, plus the help of SS survivors stationed inside Dachau.

"If we attack in such a manner as to catch the partisans off-guard, swollen with pride as they must be from their apparent victory and surely quite careless as a result," he told his superior, "then our surviving troopers inside who, until now, have been prisoners, can strike back, if only with their bare hands."

"We will have those Jews sandwiched between us!" Himmler exclaimed, seeing the worth of what was being sketched for him.

"Those Jews grabbed one of our main camps right out from under us," Rommel reminded him. "It may not be as easy as we would like."

"If we lose half a dozen men and yet destroy *them*, it will be worthwhile."

Rommel detested the notion that *any* loss of life was negligible, as though sheer mathematics somehow would nullify the impact of that loss upon the families left behind. Over the past few years, he had spoken to too many grieving loved ones about the battlefield deaths of their sons, their husbands, their brothers, their friends, and had seen that even the greatest victories were always reduced from grand, sweeping military tactics to the common denominator of a distraught mother, wife, or other family member facing a life cloaked in loss that time could only diminish but never overcome.

Rommel glanced at Himmler, who stood a head taller than himself.

I wonder if you have had to face any of that, he thought, *that dreaded collapse into tears and screams of anguish as lives are turned into nightmares?*

Himmler interrupted his thoughts.

"You command the men," he said. "I shall help any way I can."

Rommel sensed that this was less a generous gesture than a continued acknowledgement of the other man's habit of leaving the battle maneuvers to the veteran soldiers and, when successful, grabbing the credit for himself.

"Thank you, Heinrich," he replied. "Your confidence in me is inspiring."

"It is well-deserved," Himmler said a bit cryptically.

The scheme Rommel had in mind proved to be remarkably similar to the plan followed by the partisans. The SS troopers would split up into three groups, one to attack from the west, another from the south, the third from the east ends of Dachau.

"They must have used the tunnels," Rommel reasoned. "But with the apparent collapse of at least some part of it, as we have seen, it is unlikely that we can turn their own surprise against them by getting into the camp that way. We will have to station men in the alleys between the buildings."

"And at your command, they will start firing?" Himmler anticipated.

"But only after I have sent a handful of troopers up to the guard towers, where any gunfire will have been immediately preceded by grenades being thrown into the center of Dachau, one after the other, as many as they can possibly toss in rapid succession. This will create confusion among the partisans."

"And those Jews will have no idea of the size of the force hitting them . . ." Himmler mused before adding, "Brilliant, Erwin! . . . very much what I expected of you."

Is there any kind of brilliance involved when the course of action outlined is in truth the only one available? Rommel wondered cynically to himself. *How hollow this man's words surely were from the very beginning. The nation and so many of us in allegiance to it must have been suffering from some collective blindness ever to think otherwise!*

With Reichsführer Heinrich Himmler by his side, General Field Marshal Erwin Rommel gave the men their orders.

Fifteen minutes later, the Germans began their counterattack, and within half an hour had nearly completed the recapture of Dachau.

20

They don't really hate us as much as they do the Jewish prisoners," an American pilot named Ernie Clerkin said as he stood with his four comrades. "We're still alive and not quite as bad off, I suppose . . . many of the other poor souls died long ago, even though some arrived here *after* we did. I think the Nazis may want bargaining chips at some point, and they have been stockpiling American guys here and at other camps."

Still, each man looked as though he had been reduced to a near-animalistic level because of the conditions in which all had been forced to live. They all smelled of sweat and dried body wastes. Bloodshot eyes floated in skull cavities beneath pale, splotched skin stretched tight from malnutrition. Their upper torsos, visible beneath torn or shredded shirts, showed vivid bruises and scars as well as fresh cuts and a few gashes. Their legs, in the tattered prison pajamas, seemed bony and thin. Nearly all their fingernails were missing, leaving behind blood-caked sores.

"Are you able to handle weapons?" Bartlett asked.

All affirmed that they could.

The American was carrying two extra pistols plus three knives and four grenades, all of these strapped to various parts of his body. Then there were the weapons left on the floor in the main laboratory section of the medical center.

"Take these," he said, handing them everything but one gun, a knife, and a grenade. "I'll go back in and see what I can scrounge—"

A woman's voice interrupted him.

"Not necessary!" Lina Heydrich declared, smiling, as she stood in the doorway. "Many armaments are already cached in a closet at one end of the laboratory. They may be all you will need for the time being."

Bartlett's mouth dropped open as he saw that she was holding several items, ready to hand them out.

"Who *is* she?" Clerkin asked with great appreciation, and not much less awareness of her physical attributes. "Is this an angel in human disguise?"

Bartlett chuckled at that one.

"It's a very long story," he assured Clerkin.

"Tell me later, when we're safe."

The pilots rushed as quickly as they were able toward the open closet that Lina Heydrich indicated.

After grabbing all that he could handle, adrenaline moving to take the place of the weakness he suffered from confinement, Clerkin stopped for a moment in front of Mengele, who was lapsing into unconsciousness.

"That couldn't be Josef—?" he started to ask, his eyes widening as he realized that it *was* the death doctor of Auschwitz.

"I'm afraid you've guessed right, Ernie," Bartlett admitted.

"We can't just take care of him now?"

"That's what the Nazis would do. *We* mustn't allow ourselves to act like there's no difference between us."

"But he might get away. He—"

"Even if he does, Ernie, someday he'll be caught and put on trial. Let's make an example of Mengele when the time's right, with full press coverage so nobody can claim they didn't know about it."

"I hear he tried to sew two Gypsy children together—they weren't more than eleven years old—in an experiment to create Siamese twins. Can we risk the slightest chance that he *won't* be punished?"

As Bartlett was hesitating, the ground shook from multiple explosions.

Lina Heydrich hurried to the front of the building and glanced through a shattered window frame.

"I can see Heinrich Himmler and Field Marshal Rommel standing in the middle of the camp," she immediately called back to them. "More than a dozen of what I presume to be partisans are having their hands tied behind their backs. Someone next to them, a trooper, is gesturing toward this building! *Leave right now or it will be too late, please!*"

The group of six men, one woman, and an eight-year-old boy began to file out the back door, intending to cut through the barbed-wire fence only a hundred feet in front of them and head to a rendezvous point that had been prearranged. There they could link up with one of the partisans who remained behind with a vehicle, *if* he had decided to stay there after seeing through his binoculars what had been happening at Dachau.

Bartlett turned and yelled to the widow of Reinhard Heydrich, "You can still come with us. I promise you'll be treated well by the Allies."

"My children!" she reminded him. "How could I ever be expected to leave without them, no matter what you might think of me otherwise? We will live together or we will die together, whatever the case may be."

"But you won't get another chance. Arrangements could be made also to get them out of the country."

Her body language and tone of voice registered contempt.

"I will *not* become a human trophy to be trotted out by any bunch of Jew lovers for their propagandistic advantages!" she screamed. "Get out of my sight *now* . . . before I change my mind about all of this!"

Bartlett nodded, waved to her with his good arm, and then was gone with the rest.

Lina felt relieved that the American had heeded her, leaving before he was able to glimpse the tears that were coming from her eyes.

No one must ever see me this way, she told herself. *They must hate me or fear me but nothing else!*

She shifted her attention to Josef Mengele as he started to regain consciousness, possessing enough strength to rise to his elbows, leaning on them as he looked at her in astonishment.

"How . . . could . . . you . . . do . . . this?" he demanded of her, his voice strained. "Jew-loving scum like that . . . are . . . getting away. . . . What is wrong with your head, woman, for allowing this craziness to happen?"

"There is a better question," she remarked curtly.

"Better? What . . . are . . . you . . . saying?"

"Simply this, Josef, a profound dilemma: How can I allow a human devil like you to remain *alive*?"

Mengele tried to back away from her as she walked slowly toward him after bending down and picking up a nearby scalpel that was smeared with blood.

"Josef, I am afraid to say," Lina Heydrich added, "it is quite unlikely you will be inclined to applaud my answer."

They made it through the barbed wire. But then, facing them was a main highway only a few hundred feet away from Dachau.

"One by one," Bartlett told the others.

"Your wife and son first," Ernie Clerkin insisted.

That would have been Bartlett's first inclination, too, but he worried about how it would look to the men.

The others joined with Clerkin.

"We'll be right behind them," one of them assured him. "They'll be in good hands until you make it."

First Natalie ran across the highway.

On both sides were tall bushes and trees, intended to keep any observer from seeing into the camp. Ironically, these became excellent shelter for those trying to escape.

Then it was Andrew's turn.

He was in the middle of the road when a military vehicle careened around a corner at high speed, apparently heading for Dachau's entrance, which was just beyond that spot.

Andrew stood still, transfixed by the sight of the jeep with three SS troopers inside. In seconds the vehicle would hit him.

He started to run the rest of the way across, toward the trees.

Suddenly the brakes were slammed and tires squealed. The jeep lurched forward for a moment, then came to a stop.

One of the three troopers grabbed Andrew.

"Jew?" he spat out in German.

Andrew shook his head.

"What are you, boy?" the trooper demanded.

Andrew could say nothing further. He knew he dared not admit he was an American.

The trooper slapped the boy across the face.

"Let him alone, you—!" Bartlett shouted instinctively but stupidly, as he started to jump to his feet. Clerkin jerked him back, pulling on Bartlett's wounded arm. Bartlett yelped with pain but stopped and quickly pulled out his pistol with the other hand.

"I kill the young one if you interfere!" the trooper growled, startled by the fact that he and his comrades were not as alone as they had thought.

Holding his rifle with his left hand as he braced the barrel against his hip, the trooper grasped Andrew's neck with the other.

Stephen Bartlett was the first to fire, soon joined by Clerkin and another pilot.

Two of the three troopers dropped immediately. The third was the one who had grabbed Andrew. He had been hit in the face but the wound, despite the bleeding, was superficial.

Clutching his own rifle while lifting the boy up from the ground to use him as a shield, the trooper inched around the jeep toward the driver's side.

Bartlett aimed a rifle at the man's head. Andrew was tall for his age, and reached to just above the man's chin.

If my aim isn't precise, his father thought, sweat stinging his eyes and playing havoc with his vision as his finger tightened carefully around the trigger, *if—*

"Stephen, let me do it!" Clerkin whispered frantically. "You aren't steady enough to sight him accurately right now."

"No!" Bartlett told him. "I *will* do this!"

The SS trooper was now shoving Andrew into the front seat of the jeep. For a split second, he would have to let go in order to start the stalled vehicle again, while still holding his rifle in the other hand.

As this happened, Bartlett jumped up, yelling, "Now, Andrew, *now!"*

His son bolted across the front seat and shot out the other side, dropping instantly to the road and yelping as stones cut into the palms of his hands.

With no time to aim down its long barrel, the trooper threw the rifle to one side and whipped out a pistol, ready to fire as he started to duck behind the jeep, not knowing there were partisans on both sides of the road.

Too late.

Bartlett's shot hit him just below the temple, the bullet ricocheting upward, sending multiple bone fragments along with it into his brain.

Inside Dachau, the partisans had been forced to surrender. As could be expected, Rommel's tactics were superior, catching the Jews by surprise while freeing the remaining SS troopers assigned to the camp to attack any way they could manage. Partisans were either struck down by rifle fire from the force that had taken up positions inside the southern and western perimeters or were beaten, strangled, or knifed to death. They lost 60 percent of their men; the remaining 40 percent surrendered.

Himmler paraded in front of them, taunting each one, spitting into the faces of several.

"Are you *surprised* that we won?" he snarled. "Aryans against Jews . . . there can be no surprise in *that!*"

He turned to Rommel and was about to speak when the sound of gunfire stopped him.

From the direction of the medical building . . .

Rommel immediately ordered a dozen troopers to join him as he ran toward the sound. Himmler put an assistant in charge of the prisoners, then hurried along with the others.

Rommel kicked open the front door and saw Lina Heydrich standing over Josef Mengele. Apparently she had just dropped a scalpel and was turning away from him. Mengele folded his hands over his face, sobbing.

"We heard shots," Himmler spoke.

"The American pilots have escaped, along with Stephen Bartlett and his family," the widow replied.

"How long ago did they leave?" Himmler demanded.

"Less than five minutes."

"What direction, Frau Heydrich?"

Before she could reply, Mengele staggered to his feet.

"There!" he cried out, pain evident in his voice.

Rommel ordered one of the troopers to stay behind and help with Mengele while the rest, led by Himmler and himself, headed out the back exit.

Directly ahead, the barbed wire had been cut. Beyond it they could see the Americans disappearing into the woods. Only Stephen Bartlett remained visible as he ran across the main road paralleling Dachau.

His wife and son were waiting for him at the edge of the trees.

"Shoot him!" Himmler ordered.

The troopers raised their rifles.

"No," Rommel intruded. "No, that should not be done."

Himmler spun around on one heel.

"I have ordered it!" he exclaimed.

"Then do it yourself."

Rommel was under no delusion that he was doing anything but coming close to the bare edge of humiliating the other man before twelve SS troopers with possibly loose mouths. Any sharp disagreements he and Himmler had had previously in private were potentially dangerous enough, given Himmler's well-known vicious nature, but they had been miniscule in comparison to what was going on now.

Himmler grabbed a rifle and rushed forward, shouting at the American.

"Stay where you are, Stephen Bartlett!" he said as he raised the weapon. "I have waited a long time for such a moment."

He felt someone brush against his side.

"But *I* have waited just as long," Lina Heydrich spoke, "and I have far more reason."

"Then you should be the one," Himmler deferred.

He handed the rifle to her.

As she took it without hesitation, Bartlett seized the opportunity and turned to run into the surrounding shelter of ancient trees.

"Quick!" Himmler screamed.

Smiling, she aimed the rifle, though it was quite heavy for someone of her size and a frame wasted by months of mourning, placing the barrel's tip instead against the temple of Heinrich Himmler.

"No one is going to do *anything* until the American and his family are gone from here!" she declared.

"You cannot hold out for long," Himmler, infuriated, reminded her. "That rifle is heavy. You will not have the—"

"Strength?" she interrupted. "Little women such as I are so helpless compared with men, is that what you meant?"

Her free hand lashed out and in one motion opened the holster at Himmler's hip. She took out his Luger, then threw the rifle to one side.

"But, surely, even a *woman* is able to do some harm with a weapon of *this* caliber, would you not agree?" she called out so everyone could hear what she was saying, her tone deliberately drained of emotion.

A number of minutes passed.

"You are letting the enemy escape!" Himmler bellowed.

"If you are telling me that the enemy can be a man who simply wants to save his wife and his son from the horrors of *this* camp, then, yes, I *shall* let them *escape!* I would rather die from a hundred bullets than put any of them through—"

"The very one who participated in the plot that brought about the death of your own husband," Himmler interrupted. "He helped to deprive *your* children of the kind of father they deserve as proud Aryan offspring."

Lina Heydrich hesitated, memories of the early years of her marriage spinning through her mind with the frenzy of a kaleidoscope. Suddenly those scenes were replaced by others, a man who had become degraded by the regime he served.

"*You* and the band of devils to which you belong murdered my beloved long before any assassins reached him!" she spat out the words. "Reinhard *learned* to hate. He was not always that way. *You* cleverly taunted him with the possibility that he might have Jewish blood in his veins. To make him hate *that,* you seduced him with a vision straight out of hell!"

"It is interesting that you despise me so much *now,*" Himmler retorted, aware of how many ears were listening to her words. "There was a time when you felt much more warmly toward me, Frau Heydrich."

"Perhaps once. . . ." she admitted musingly. "I suppose it might have been that the two of you corrupted one another. Who can say? I know only one truth . . . what I saw inside that camp."

She tilted her head slightly, as though listening for a moment to some voice within it.

"My children are *my* children," she said then. "But Dachau can only be *your* child. I hold *my* children in my arms, and I feel their warmth. What do *you* feel when you see Dachau and Treblinka and Auschwitz and all the others?"

Finally, weary, and saddened, Lina Heydrich seemed about ready to lower the pistol when the sounds of noisy movement came from inside the medical building.

Rommel jerked around and saw someone in the doorway propping himself against the framework.

"No!" Rommel screamed. "You cannot—!"

Abruptly, a shot rang out.

Lina Heydrich's face contorted, and she let out a sudden cry as she tottered and fell, the cream-colored blouse she wore rapidly turning red.

Josef Mengele, his own clothes stained with blood, stood in the doorway, the pistol he held emitting a thin stream of smoke that was gone in an instant.

"I *had* to shoot her," he blathered.

Rommel dashed over to him and grabbed the gun out of his hand.

"What else was I to do?" Mengele pleaded, his face draining of any color that had been left before he crumpled to the ground.

"If she dies, so do you!" Rommel yelled as he stood over the man. "We do not shoot the widows of our war heroes, no matter what the provocation."

He heard Himmler order troopers across the highway and into the woods. But just then, filled with anger and disgust so intense that he found it hard to breathe, Rommel had very little thought for anything but the nation for which he once would have been willing to die, and the terrible days he saw ahead.

21

The heavyset, balding partisan was dressed more like a farmer than a Resistance fighter. Earlier, Anton Littman had been designated as one of the four men serving at lookout posts, each placed at a spot facing a different corner of Dachau.

Now Littman was getting into the truck parked near the base of the tree that he had been using as a vantage point.

"Wait!" Bartlett shouted while he ran ahead, trying to get his attention.

Littman let the motor idle as he jumped out of the cab and hugged the American.

"I thought everyone was doomed!" he exclaimed. "I thought I would be driving an empty truck."

"Let's go—quickly! But not back to the cave," Bartlett told him.

"Why, Stephen? Our comrades are there."

"Someone betrayed them—and us. I suspect it might have been Gustav Dobrik. I doubt that it was Felix Kellar."

"So you are saying there is probably nothing for us back there? We are very much alone, is that it?"

"I think the Nazis would be careful to preserve the *illusion* of something as you approached, a nominal group kept at the cave to make it look as though all is well, but nothing more than that, Anton."

"And Gestapo or SS troopers waiting in the shadows!" Littman said as he threw up his hands in exasperation.

His attention turned to the pilots, the woman and the boy who were waiting a few feet behind Bartlett.

"Are they Americans?" he asked, pointing to the men, since it was obvious who the others were.

"Yes . . ."

"Secretly taken captive and being held as, how do you say it, ah, yes, aces up the Nazis' sleeves?"

"Exactly, my friend."

Littman frowned, his expression intent.

"Where do we go now, Stephen?"

"Switzerland. It offers our only chance."

"But the border entry points are heavily guarded on the German side."

"Yes, I know. But I have something else in mind. You see, I was in Switzerland not long before war broke out, Anton."

"What were you doing there?" Littman asked.

"I hate to admit it, but something as simple as skiing."

Littman had no idea where the American was heading.

"So what did you find out?" he asked dumbly.

"That there is a little-known resort-type hotel on the slopes of the Alps just at the edge of the border with Germany. It was built in the early 1930s by wealthy—"

The American's face evidenced his discomfort at finishing that sentence.

"Jews? Is that not correct?" Littman interceded quickly, trying to ease the way the other man undoubtedly felt.

Bartlett nodded.

"Do not feel awkward about speaking the truth, Stephen. Not even the Nazis could have ascended to power *completely* on a foundation of falsehoods. Many of my fellow Jews *did* take advantage of Germany's financially prostrate position more than a decade ago."

Clearing his throat, Bartlett went on, ignoring that last sentence, which seemed so close to Nazi dogma. "When Switzerland declared neutrality and the Final Solution began in earnest, I am sure the Nazis closed it down."

Littman's shoulders slumped as he replied, "So, how does that help us? I fail to understand what you are getting at. The only miracle here would be if Almighty God handed us a cable car and—"

His eyes widened as he saw the smile on the American's face.

"Tell me, please, Stephen, that you *are* going to say what I am *praying* you will," Littman begged.

"From the German side across *into* Switzerland!" Bartlett exclaimed gladly. "I'm sure it is quite deserted. I can't believe the Nazis have been foolish enough to waste manpower guarding it."

"But, in that case, the motors running the lift surely have not been kept in repair," Littman protested, his pragmatic side kicking in as he thought of that unfortunate but nonetheless real possibility.

"Ah, but the cables almost certainly remain," the American pointed out.

Frightening images danced across Anton Littman's mind, suppressed fears from childhood confronting him.

"This may not be such a miracle after all," he moaned, having lapsed into a heavily Yiddish accent.

"One thing is certain," Bartlett reminded him. "It's all we have."

Lina Heydrich and Josef Mengele both were quickly flown to Berlin where the two of them received emergency medical care. Heinrich Himmler and Erwin Rommel remained briefly at Dachau, waiting until a fresh group of SS troopers could be dispatched from the nearest military installation.

Those in pursuit of Bartlett, his family, and the escaped pilots had to return without having captured anyone. They encountered little more than tire tracks in the dirt and footprints that led north, south, east, and west away from Dachau.

"It was very well planned," Himmler was told. "We could not be certain which direction to go. And there were not enough of us to split up and continue after them. Do you have any further instructions for us, sir?"

Himmler shook his head and ordered the men to rejoin the others.

A short while later, Himmler elected to be flown back to Berlin, ostensibly in order to return to his official duties as quickly as possible after so much time and energy had been diverted from them.

But Rommel suspected otherwise, having seen his superior's discomfort increasing the longer he was exposed to the resumption of camp life as it had been for more than ten years at Dachau, brutal and degrading, a level of existence that Himmler had decreed long before but seldom came face-to-face with. The camps were often given something of a facelift just before he was scheduled to visit one or the other. In time he would be given singular credit for the Final Solution, but devising a grand plan and seeing the results of it would prove devastating to the man, especially since nothing had been done to "dress up" Dachau this time. Under the circumstances it was wholly unprepared for his visit.

Nevertheless, Himmler did nothing to mitigate the punishment meted out to the partisans who were now prisoners along with those already confined who had taken part in the hostilities—who, as far as commandant Richard Gluecks was concerned, happened to be everyone.

Finally, Himmler was ready to return to Berlin.

"I shall remain here with the troops," Rommel said, barely able to conceal his disgust. "They need a leader, and I am happy to be the one who accompanies them back . . . if that is all right with you."

Himmler nodded weakly, his features even more pale-looking than usual. He seemed unsteady on his feet as he boarded the helicopter. Turning for an instant, his eyes bloodshot, Hitler's Grand Inquisitor, as some called him, allowed a fleeting expression of admiration mixed with an odd hint of longing to settle on his face as he gave a farewell salute. Then it was gone, that fragile moment of humanity, and he disappeared inside.

"Sir?" a trooper came to him a few seconds later.

"Yes?" Rommel asked as he studied the young man standing in front of him.

"I am very glad that we do not have to stay here any longer."

"You are?"

"It is an awful place. I am not so certain I could have—"

The man sensed that he was revealing too intimate a glimpse of his feelings, and he stopped, staring at his boots instead.

Rommel placed a hand on his shoulder.

"Never, never be ashamed of what you have told me," he said, smiling kindly. "But *always* be careful to whom you say it."

The young trooper nodded and awkwardly excused himself.

Please, God, Rommel prayed silently, without anyone suspecting. *Let this war be ended before they lay claim to his soul as well.*

Minutes later, the convoy rolled out of Dachau through the main entrance. Rommel read the words in metal letters over it: *Arbeit macht frei.* His hands doubled into fists until blood seeped from his palms as the nails cut into them.

Arbeit macht frei . . . Work brings freedom.

The thick, heavy wooden gates shut behind him like the doors to some huge mausoleum, as though the men inside were already dead.

DEADLY SANCTION

Field Marshal Erwin Rommel drew his black leather overcoat more tightly around him, a sudden, deep chill overtaking him.

They were near the southern border of Germany. Ahead of them was the northern-most section of the Alps. If they could make their way across, they could meet up with partisans in Basel, Switzerland. From there, the entire group, with the exception of Anton Littman who wanted to remain behind, could attempt clandestine contact with the Allied command center in London.

Littman had chosen back roads, reasoning that the Nazis would continue to ignore these since their manpower was stretched thin along the entire front lines as the war turned against them.

Often the truck was forced to travel on simple footpaths.

Two miles from their destination, it plunged partway into a shallow unseen ditch, and the rear axle broke.

They would have to walk the rest of the way. Everyone needed to carry weapons or ammunition, the latter falling in part to Natalie and Andrew Bartlett.

It was a beautiful time, an autumn as colorful as anyone could imagine but also with hint of the cold temperatures that would soon accompany blankets of snow.

"We walk through a wonderland," Ernie Clerkin acknowledged, "but there is no time to stop and look at the beauty."

"A coffin," Littman pointed out. "If the Nazis find us, we might end up being buried in all these leaves."

Clerkin sighed as he nodded.

"How tragic for you and your people," he said, "to live in such a country, and then to have it ripped out from under you."

"We are Germans, too," Littman told him. "The Nazis always forget that. We were born here just as they were. We love *Deutschland* every bit as much as they claim to do."

Bartlett wondered how many times Littman had thought or spoken those words, for he seemed to be saying them as though by rote.

Ahead, through a clearing in the overhead branches, Stephen Bartlett spied a peak.

"There it is!" he exclaimed. "The buildings are on the other side."

"I think I see the cable," Clerkin said, stopping for a moment to look through binoculars. "That's it! Still there!"

Littman was using another pair.

"Look how far it extends," he said, his voice trembling. "If the cable car fails to work, we will need so much strength to get across."

Bartlett didn't relish that idea, either. He knew that he could make it but then he wondered about his wife and son, especially because they had just gone through their ordeal at Dachau. And what about the pilots who had been confined to the camp for a much longer period?

Lord, Lord, let it be in good shape, please, please let the cable car be in working condition! he prayed.

"Stephen?" Littman asked. "Were you praying just then?"

Bartlett nodded.

"How did you know?"

"You walked differently," the other man observed. "Your head was slightly bowed, your eyes half-closed. It was not difficult for me to guess."

"Only God can get us through this, Anton."

"We share the same faith, Stephen," Littman remarked.

"You are a Christian?" Bartlett asked, surprised.

"I consider myself a completed Jew."

"Were the others aware?"

"I never told them. Some were very devout Jews. They would have been greatly offended. What has happened is between God and me."

The two men hugged one another and then continued up the trail.

The resort was a complex of buildings on two plateaus naturally cut into the side of the mountain.

"It's exactly as I remembered it," Bartlett told everyone.

They all had gotten a quick glimpse of the hotel before turning around a corner of the mountain's base, which now blocked it from view.

Clerkin offered to reconnoiter the site.

"What is there to search out?" Littman asked, throwing up his hands. "I thought you said it was deserted, Stephen."

"Being careful is better than being caught, Anton," the American replied. "Perhaps the Nazis decided to use it as a makeshift storage depot; who knows?"

Clerkin was already walking ahead, not eager to be caught in any argument between the two men. He disappeared around an outjutting section of the mountain.

The rest waited.

Littman was becoming more impatient.

"We must do something soon!" he protested again. "The longer we wait, the more chance we have of being spotted by a passing patrol."

Bartlett was beginning to feel that the other man was right.

He checked his watch.

Fifteen minutes.

Clerkin had been gone—

They heard sounds, a man panting.

Suddenly Clerkin rejoined them.

"Everything *is* in working order!" he exclaimed as he tried to catch his breath.

"Wonderful," Bartlett responded. "That's great news."

Clerkin was shaking his head.

"It isn't, Stephen," he said. "It's not great news at all. The equipment—the cable car, an enclosed swimming pool, the lights, *everything*—is working just fine *because this place has become a retreat for Gestapo and SS officers!*"

He was shaking as he spoke, tears commencing.

"As much as I can tell, there are a dozen of them present right now, including—"

Ernie Clerkin almost choked as he told them, *"—Adolf Hitler himself!"*

22

Stephen Bartlett stood on a ledge overlooking the second plateau. He was staring directly into a large room. Through an oversized picture window, he could glimpse half a dozen men gathered around a floor-to-ceiling chiseled-stone fireplace. On the walls hung a variety of stuffed animal heads to which they pointed periodically and laughed.

"I don't see anyone in there who looks at all like Hitler," he admitted to Clerkin, who was just behind him.

"I'm not going crazy, Stephen," the other protested.

"I think we should go back now. We've got a huge problem here, Ernie. It's more important than—"

"*Look!*" Clerkin exclaimed as he gazed through a pair of binoculars.

Bartlett used his own.

"Where?" he asked, irritated now.

"In the center . . . the shorter man in the gray uniform."

"He must have turned around. I see only his back, Ernie."

"Wait! Look now!"

The little man turn slowly.

Bartlett saw the little moustache in the center of his top lip, saw the thin patch of hair on his head, saw the robot-like body motions in the sudden outstretching of his arms, the cold seriousness of his facial movements.

The Führer *himself!*

Bartlett's own face seemed bloodless as he said, "There must be other Gestapo agents all over this area. I don't see how it could be otherwise. The Nazis aren't fools. What in the world have we stumbled into?"

"An outpost of hell, Stephen . . . and the devil incarnate is only a few hundred yards in front of us!"

Both men shivered at the thought.

"We need to talk to the others," Bartlett pointed out. "I think I know what we at least have to consider doing now. And it will require everyone's consent and cooperation."

It was then, more than any other time, that he wished he had not become the *de facto* leader of that small group and, therefore, the man who would have to make the most crucial decision of his lifetime. If someone had been in charge, he could disagree and, if necessary, not go along. But he, as their leader, could hardly postulate a course of action upon which he himself was not prepared to set out.

"You and I probably have the same idea," Clerkin suggested, studying his fellow American and arriving at the same point himself. "Along with the men, it surely would mean sacrificing your family as well."

"Am I all that transparent, Ernie?"

"Just tell me: Am I right?"

"If you're thinking of . . ."

Bartlett didn't want to say what he knew he must.

Oh, Lord, to get them out of Dachau, and to be so close to safety . . . yet come up against this! But there's nothing else to do, is there? We have only one choice.

"Could we do it, Ernie?" he asked finally, still not able to say the words.

"I think we could. They're not expecting any attack. This whole business, I bet, is supposed to be a secret, as far as they are concerned. It's a hideaway for them to relax, to enjoy a little luxury without the sacrificing populace ever finding them out."

Bartlett nodded in agreement.

"Then we must tell the others," he said.

"I wish there were another way, Stephen. If we fail, my family back in the States will survive. But for you, that may not be the case.

"There isn't an alternative, a viable one, though. I know that. Hitler is so close. Whatever the consequences, we *have* to kill him."

Clerkin started back to the alcove in the mountainside where the others were waiting, Bartlett following him.

Though an autumn chill had become evident, Stephen Bartlett felt oppressively warm, every inch of his hefty body soaked with perspiration. After going through so much to free his wife and his son, now he had decided that, first, a man responsible for the deaths of millions of people would have to be killed before their safety could be considered. Thus Bartlett, himself, would place their lives in jeopardy once again.

Or Hitler could be captured! he thought abruptly.

That notion hit him hard, and he stopped walking.

Clerkin sensed this, turned around, asked, "Stephen, what's wrong?"

"We've failed to consider one other possibility that is no less hazardous but a different one, anyway," Bartlett spoke.

"What are you saying?"

"Take Hitler *alive!*"

"That's ridiculous. How could we—?"

Clerkin rubbed his chin, the idea taking hold.

"Get him into Switzerland somehow, deliver him to the partisans," he spoke with increasing enthusiasm, "and then try and persuade them to let the Allies take over from there. Am I correct, Stephen?"

"Right on the money, Ernie. In wartime, kidnapping becomes thinkable, an action that would never be sanctioned at any other time."

"If the generals who hate Hitler and want to depose him could be tipped off *before* Himmler and the rest can be told anything about the chaos that would follow, they could move into the vacuum and take over."

"And I know two generals who would be ideal for such a task!"

"Rommel, I bet, is one of them. Who else?"

Even with a man such as Ernie Clerkin seemed to be, who admittedly was little more than a stranger, Bartlett knew he could not allow himself to blow the cover of Henning von Tresckow, someone who had essentially become the primary force behind any clandestine planning by German military figures to assassinate the Führer.

There were no objections to what Bartlett told them. He had half-expected Natalie to protest, but what she did say made him love her all the more.

"I saw women in Dachau, women whose sons and daughters had ended up in ditches nearby after being dragged away from them," she spoke, everyone listening. "Lime was poured over their little bodies. I heard stories about the Nazis planting the seeds or bulbs of flowers in the soil after it had been thrown back on top of the bodies. One of the guards joked, 'At least we can get *something* worthwhile out of the *Juden!*'"

She glanced quickly from man to man.

"If we could do something to stop this, to cut short the horror, I think we *must*, whatever the costs to ourselves."

Assent came from everybody else.

"So we're together on this then," Bartlett confirmed. "We go after the Führer."

He noticed Littman, who was standing to one side with a worried expression on his face; a moment later, Bartlett walked over to the man.

"Are you all right?" he asked.

"Yes . . . ," Littman replied, speaking quite slowly. "In a manner of speaking, I suppose you could say that I am."

He shook his head as though to rid it of mental cobwebs.

"My people have hated this man for so long, and now he is only a short distance away. One part of me wants him dead, *very* dead, Stephen."

His manner turning curiously sheepish, Littman added, "But I agree with you that he could be of far more use alive than as a corpse. I promise you this, my friend: that you will get no more static from me!"

The two men shook hands.

Nevertheless, Bartlett was not thoroughly convinced about Littman. Something seemed remotely unsettling about the man, perhaps because he was so quickly willing to go along with the kidnapping and, in the process, bury his apparent desire for vengeance.

But I can't allow intangibles to distract me, Bartlett thought. *More important is the little man with the moustache.*

Yet deciding to kidnap Adolf Hitler was the easy part. Figuring out *how* to do it came next.

The Gestapo agents patrolling the grounds, several on the bottom plateau and the one just above it, were killed, either knifed or their necks broken, dragged behind boulders, their voices stifled so that they could not scream a warning.

"What we're able to do . . . it seems so easy!" Ernie Clerkin exclaimed as he dropped another man at his feet. "How can that be, with Adolf Hitler in there, Stephen? How can it be going on like this?"

"I know," Bartlett agreed. "That bothers me as much as it does you."

"You said it! Whatever we might think about the morality of Gestapo tactics, they *have* been trained as a vicious group. But these guys are no contest at all."

It was the same with two SS troopers they encountered— a brief struggle and the troopers were dead.

"Could they be doing what they would certainly have no compunction about doing? Sacrificing young, green manpower?" Clerkin mused. "That sort of thing never bothered them before now."

"To throw us off-guard?" Bartlett offered.

"Think about it, Stephen. That's a possibility, you know. Their hardened pros might be inside waiting for us . . . a classic Nazi trap."

Bartlett ran those words through his mind one more time.

"Which means they would have been tipped off," he said, disgusted by the prospect. "But when? And by whom, Ernie?"

Clerkin slapped the palm of his left hand against his forehead.

"But the Führer, Stephen! If they knew in advance, would they have kept him in such a position of danger? That part doesn't make sense."

Bartlett agreed, but thought of something else.

"Unless—" he started to say.

He did not get to finish his sentence. The sound of an exploding grenade shattered the quiet of that isolated spot.

Coming from the two-level resort building . . .

"What the h—?" Clerkin shouted, jolted.

Sounds of confusion came from inside.

"We've got to attack now," Bartlett said. "Whatever the cause, it's given us an opening we might not have again."

"I'll go around back and tell the men there."

"I'll take care of the front."

Three minutes later, the attack had started. Two minutes after that, they were inside the building.

Anton Littman had broken away from the rest of the group and had tried to get into the building through a rear entrance. The grenade he used to blow it open took a large chunk out of that entire side.

Through the haze of ensuing smoke and dust caused by scattered debris, he saw several men hurrying to that part of the building. He threw another grenade that tossed them to one side or the other.

Then he charged inside, wielding in his left hand a Mauser Model 712 Schnellfeuer and in his right hand, a long-barrel version of the Walther Armee-Pistole.

The attack from the front caught the Germans inside as much by surprise as the one from the rear. Littman's onslaught was so intense that it led them to assume that more than one man was involved. As the Germans resisted, one of the American pilots was killed but four Germans perished, too, and another was wounded, collapsing among a pile of debris not far from where Littman had succeeded in entering.

Finally, after only a few minutes, they surrendered.

Littman stood in the middle of the main room, the one where earlier the Führer had been seen. His Mauser was pressed against the head of the personification of evil he had decided must be killed.

"No!" Bartlett said, walking toward him. "We need him alive. We can do much more if he is kept—"

"You are not someone who has lost family and friends because of this monster!" Littman screamed. "You have your loved ones with you even now, Stephen. This devil should not be granted one more second of life."

His finger pressed more tightly against the trigger of the weapon as tears started to stream down his cheeks.

"*Stephen!*" a trembling, somewhat familiar voice penetrated the momentary silence after Littman had spoken.

Bartlett spun around at the mention of his name.

"*Do . . . not . . . let . . . this . . . happen!*" the voice groaned.

The wounded German!

Bartlett had passed the crumpled form in the German general's black uniform without stopping.

He now hurried to the other man's side, bending down and wiping dust and dirt from his thin, angular face.

Henning von Tresckow!

"*Do . . . not . . . harm . . . him!*" his old friend begged. "*Stephen . . . you . . . cannot . . . allow . . . this chance to . . . slip . . . away . . . from . . . us!*"

He struggled to his elbows, waving frantically at Littman as he called out, "*You must stop! That . . . is . . . not . . . the . . . Führer.*"

"Liar!" Littman shouted back, overhearing what von Tresckow had been saying. "He dies *now!*"

He blew the man's head apart, then dropped his weapons, his shoulders slumping as he started to sob violently.

Henning von Tresckow grabbed Bartlett's jacket.

"We . . . had . . . located . . . a perfect double . . . we were going to poison the real Hitler and substitute . . . this one!"

He managed to struggle to his feet, then staggered toward Littman.

"You bloody fool!" he said, his face dark red with anger. *"You—"*

Littman grabbed von Tresckow by the neck and started to choke him.

"We have *earned* the privilege," Littman said. "A million Jews, two, three million, cry out from their graves for just what I have done. I spit on your treachery!"

Ernie Clerkin jumped in, grabbed Littman, and pulled him away while Bartlett held von Tresckow to keep him from falling against some of the rubble.

"Oh, Stephen . . . ." von Tresckow groaned. *"My friend, my friend, what we have lost! What we have lost this day!"*

23

_____

After calming down, Littman walked over to von Tresckow who was sprawled on a sofa next to Bartlett. An impromptu operation by a pilot who had also had medical training retrieved the bullet that had entered his thigh. Considerable blood had been lost but there were no complications, it seemed.

"General, I am deeply, deeply sorry about what has happened," Littman spoke, an anguished expression twisting his face.

"I can hardly blame you," von Tresckow acknowledged. "After all, we desperately wanted that man to be as realistic an imperson- ation as humanly possible. You proved that we were successful."

His eyes narrowed as he looked at the other man more closely.

"This is strange, I know, but you seem so familiar to me, Mr. Littman," he said. "Is it possible that we have met before?"

"You may be thinking of a year ago when I was imprisoned by your men on one occasion, and mysteriously released a short while later. Now I can see why."

"That must be it," von Tresckow agreed, though as various images filled his mind, he was not as certain as he sounded, images of a stage and an audience sitting in front of it, with applause filling the air.

Littman shook his hand.

"I must try to reach one of the partisan groups," he said. "You seem to have quite a shortwave setup here."

Von Tresckow smiled as he replied, "Put together by bits and pieces pilfered over a period of years, I assure you."

After Littman had left, Bartlett asked, "What was that all about, Henning?"

"It is probably nothing, Stephen," von Tresckow said. "I just thought we had met before. His explanation is—"

"—not satisfactory, is it?" Bartlett interrupted.

"You have seen through me, my friend. You are quite right. But there is no valid reason to believe otherwise. And neither of us should feel at all nervous about his loyalty, if that is what concerns you."

"When you were semiconscious, you were rambling on about a stage play at a well-known theater in Berlin. The performances were so superior that even the Führer himself stood and applauded."

"Those images stay with me," von Tresckow admitted. "But there is not necessarily something sinister in this."

"So you don't feel apprehensive, then?"

"Why should I? The man thought he was killing Adolf Hitler. What greater testimony to his genuineness could there be? If you are hinting something about him, and I suspect you are, that alone should make you feel better. Nobody would dare do such a thing *unless* he hated the Führer with a great and abiding passion."

"Fine," Bartlett agreed. "We'll drop the subject."

Von Tresckow nodded as he said somberly, "I am very sorry that one of the pilots was killed, Stephen."

"But it is also a pity that four of *your* men are gone. This was an astounding charade, Henning."

"It *could* have worked, Stephen. You see, an attempt on Hitler's life is being planned at Rastenberg in July. What we wanted to do was incapacitate the devil or kill him, and then substitute the double."

"How long has this been in the works?"

"A year, perhaps more. We were in the midst of yet another rehearsal, trying to see how convincing the man was in a less tense social environment. Oh, my friend, he was doing so well, this fine actor of ours."

"He was an actor?"

"It turned out to be quite fortuitous actually. Goebbels had heard about this actor who was playing the Führer in a government-approved play out in the provinces. He knew I was going to be traveling in that vicinity, so he asked me if I would attend a performance and form an opinion about how good the man was."

"For a government-produced version at the Berlin Opera House?"

"I assumed that was the case—until I discovered the most delicious irony of all."

Von Tresckow smiled from ear to ear.

"Oh, Stephen, it would have been wonderful."

"Fill me in," Bartlett said a bit impatiently.

"*They* had had a similar purpose in mind for him."

"Using an actor in place of the Führer?"

"As an occasional decoy, yes! The assassination of Reinhard Heydrich that you were so successful in helping to bring about sent a chill through the entire Nazi hierarchy. They were eager to put in place *any* measures that would confound the enemy and become yet another obstacle to any further assassinations actually being carried out."

"But *you* got him instead. How did that happen?"

"He hated Hitler, despised what was being done to *Deutschland,* and had nothing but sympathy for the Jews and their plight. We were handed by God Himself the greatest possible friend and now . . . now . . ."

He could not talk for a few moments. Bartlett waited patiently.

"At least we can help you and your loved ones and those pilots get to a *safe* haven," von Tresckow finally said. "At least *that* opportunity will not slip between our fingers."

Von Tresckow and the rest of the conspirators had had the resort's cable-car machinery refurbished after it had fallen into disrepair since the Nazis abandoned it years before.

"We have viewed this as our escape route," he said, "in case escape became necessary, as opposed to victory."

All of it was in good shape now, and well able to transport Stephen Bartlett, his family, the remaining pilots, and Anton Littman over into Switzerland.

"I was alerted to the possibility that you might end up here," von Tresckow said matter-of-factly.

"Warned?" Bartlett repeated. "By whom?"

"Rommel."

"Is he going to cooperate with you?"

"I must say that Field Marshal Rommel is still trying to make up his mind. There is yet a part of him that equates such activity with treason, whereas *we* find the Nazis to be the ones guilty of that!"

"But then he is a man of honor. If you get him to support a plan to oust Hitler, he will do so at the risk of his own death."

"I agree. His indecision has nothing to do with lack of valor."

As the two men talked, Bartlett stood against a railing on a veranda that presented them with a panorama of snow-capped mountains and valleys adorned by chateaux that seemed like the dollhouses of playful children. Von Tresckow, his bandaged leg propped on a chair, sat nearby.

"Some portions of Bavaria are like this," the German sighed. "The air is clean. There are no sounds of warfare in the distance. No camps of dying men, women, and children exist for many, many miles."

He turned to his American friend.

"I have something quite astonishing to tell you," he said. "Although you may well dismiss it as battlefield gossip."

"If you tell me it is true, I shall accept it as such," Bartlett assured him.

"It is about Himmler."

"He's dead?"

"Nothing like that . . . much more intriguing."

Von Tresckow cleared his throat and went on, "Himmler is gradually losing influence, you know."

"That *is* astonishing!" Bartlett agreed.

"But that is only a small part of what I have learned," von Tresckow went on, his thin, aristocratic face taking on an expression of excitement. "The man has sent out feelers, Stephen, he has sent out feelers to the Allies!"

"About surrender?"

"Oh, it is much more complicated than that. Apparently he has offered to *cooperate* in deposing the Führer!"

Bartlett's mouth dropped open.

"No, I am not mad, my friend," von Tresckow said, a mischievous smile playing around his face.

"I don't doubt your sanity, Henning. It is your sources that I have to call into question."

"I have been informed by a source very close to him."

"An aide?"

"No, his wife."

"How did you convince her that you could be trusted?"

"I did not have to do that, Stephen. The woman has been involved with us for some time now. It is through her that we have been receiving some of our most valuable information."

Bartlett had to lean against the iron railing at the edge of the veranda.

"You were right when you tried to prepare me for this," he said. "I would never have imagined *any* of it."

"There is one final piece in this puzzle," von Tresckow added. "It may be the most unexpected of all."

The American was listening eagerly.

"Heinrich Himmler has offered to lead Germany, in concert with the Allies, against a threat that he is convinced has the potential to dominate the world."

"Communist Russia!"

"You are precisely right, Stephen."

"What about the fact that Germany failed in its earlier assault? What would be different this next time?"

"Hitler would not be making the decisions. Himmler and Rommel would, however."

"Rommel has been enlisted in this?"

"Not as yet. The subject has not even been discussed with Erwin. For the moment, only Churchill, Roosevelt, de Gaulle, and Himmler know . . . apart from me and a handful of my fellow plotters and, now, you."

Von Tresckow's manner turned solemn, dark.

"What is it, Henning?" Bartlett asked.

"One man stands in the way."

"Who is that?"

"Franklin Delano Roosevelt."

"Roosevelt is balking? You are telling me the president of the United States is not in favor of any of this?"

"He is a sick man, Stephen. Some say he is dying. His mind is no longer sharp. He seems more interested in appeasing the Russians than conquering them."

"He would be put in the position of betraying an ally. I suppose, now that I think of it, he may have something there."

"An ally, yes, but one determined to control half of Europe by the time the war is over," von Tresckow pointed out. "Himmler has in his possession secret intelligence documents that provide at least a hint of this. What he is trying to do is convince everyone that they would be exchanging one aggressor for another if they fail to seize the opportunity while Germany still has a fighting force of some significance."

"And a growing rocket capability, I suppose, which could be aimed toward Russian military installations," Bartlett added.

"Which is Hitler's reason for hanging on, whatever the

devastation to *Deutschland*. Now it is Himmler's as well, but for a totally different purpose."

Bartlett bowed his head.

"You've not told me the other obstacle, have you?" he spoke. "It's more than just Roosevelt, isn't it?"

"Himmler wants to be forgiven for his war crimes," von Tresckow acknowledged.

Bartlett let out his breath slowly, and it hovered in a white cloud in front of him before dissipating.

"And what happens to Goering, Goebbels, Eichmann, all the rest?"

"Himmler cares little for them," von Tresckow replied. "They are not included in the negotiations."

"Where do you stand in all of this, Henning?"

"That is a difficult issue. What we have here is something that is vaguely Christian."

"How so?"

"Heinrich Himmler wants to be forgiven his sins."

"Does he even acknowledge that he *has* sinned in the first place?"

"Implicitly, if not explicitly," von Tresckow commented. "I've seen how he reacted to the conditions at more than one camp."

"You haven't told me where you stand, my friend," Bartlett said.

"I think this man is battling whatever remains of his Roman Catholic upbringing. It took visiting Auschwitz and, now, Dachau to bring to the surface what had been buried under layers of Nazi dogma."

"So you would be inclined to grant him what he wanted?"

"We are caught between devils, my dear Stephen. Do we assume repentance in the one so we can scourge the other from our midst? I am too tired right now to plumb the depths of *that* question."

A nervous Anton Littman barged outside and interrupted them.

"We must hurry, Stephen," he said, panting, his right cheek twitching. "I just got a report over the shortwave. I think it was relayed from one of our partisan enclaves in Bavaria. Some German fighter planes have taken off from a base outside Berlin. They are supposed to be headed *in this direction!*"

24

The cable car had little room left after Ernie Clerkin squeezed in with the four pilots, Stephen Bartlett, his wife, and his son. Anton Littman offered to remain behind.

"There is no way you can afford to be drifting about in enemy territory," Bartlett insisted. "If you come with us you'll be safe in Switzerland until you can take stock of the situation and have a better plan of action."

"But there is so little room, Stephen," Littman resisted. "Can the cable car hold such weight? Who can say?"

"If an air assault is coming," von Tresckow cut in, "you can be certain that Berlin has plans for it to be joined by one from the ground also."

"All because of what you've been doing here?" Bartlett asked.

"It may not be entirely us, you know."

Bartlett knew immediately what his friend was implying.

"We broke into a major camp, freed their American prisoners, and in the process, humiliated the mighty military and internal security machine that Himmler, Heydrich, and others had worked for so many years to put together. One American and a few dozen scruffy Jews did that, so the Nazis want to get the rest of us back or slaughter everyone in the process! Their egos will hardly allow for less."

Von Tresckow grunted in agreement.

"*One* of us is the frosting on the cake, as you Americans would call it," von Tresckow. "They either are after you and we happen to be thrown in. Or they are after us as conspirators and traitors, and *you* just dropped by as a wonderful dividend for them."

"If escape is so tenuous for Anton here on the German side," Bartlett surmised, "what about you and your men?"

"We are not Jews," von Tresckow reminded him pointedly. "We have really quite a simple explanation. We take the two jeeps and the small truck that brought us here in the first place and blow them up. It will be very easy to convince any officer in charge that we were ambushed during a patrol in this area.

"I can tell them that I got a report about suspicious activity involving the double for Hitler about whom Berlin had warned us months ago. I wanted to check out the vicinity before I called in any forces. Ironically, we have more than enough casualties from your own assault to add rather grisly credence to this story."

In the distance, the sound of approaching planes intruded.

"Hurry!" von Tresckow pleaded. "Anton, get on-board *now!*"

Littman nodded, shook his hand heartily, and jumped through the entrance into the enclosed cable car.

Von Tresckow turned to one of his men and ordered him to start the motor. For a moment, it sputtered uncertainly, then the car lurched away from the side of the mountain. The two groups, one on the veranda and the other now suspended from a cable, waved to one another.

"For the love of—!" Ernie Clerkin started to exclaim.

He was looking through a pair of binoculars out of the north side of the cable car while another pilot was surveying the south side.

"Four planes," Clerkin said. "I see four German fighter planes. They'll be here in less than a minute."

The cable car was a bit more than halfway to Switzerland, having crossed a chasm that sometimes stretched as deep as five thousand feet to the valley floor, when the planes flew directly overhead. One turned slightly west and fired at the resort, scoring a direct hit and devastating much of the structure on that second plateau. Another added a second barrage. The remaining two failed to fire.

Abruptly, the cable car stopped.

"Above us!" Littman said. "Above us! I ran a machine shop. We repaired motors. I know the design of this car. There is a hand crank of sorts on top, just below the cable. It was installed as a safety feature."

He turned to Bartlett.

"Stephen, please, go up with me. We *can* do this. We've got to try."

Suddenly, the car lurched, then rolled along the cable at increasing speed. Natalie screamed, locking Andrew in a protective embrace. Then, inexplicably, the car jolted to a stop fifty feet from the Swiss terminal—and still two hundred feet from the rocky mountainside below. Everyone was knocked to the floor as the car rocked precariously.

"Something's wrong!" Littman exclaimed. "I think the cable must be old . . . too much weight on it in one spot. We *must* start moving again, or we all die if the cable snaps."

He pointed to the ceiling.

"That panel moves. We climb up through there."

Bartlett jumped once, twice, then made it on the third try; he pushed the panel aside, then pulled himself through the opening and reached down for Littman.

A short metal clamp attached the cabin to the mechanism that moved along the cable. The hand crank Littman had mentioned was visible between the clamp and the mechanism.

"There is a handle we can use," he said, raising his voice so he could be heard above the chill wind that was starting to howl between the mountain peaks on both sides of the border. "We must work as a team, Stephen. First you, then me . . . then you, then me."

"Got it!" Bartlett replied.

Bracing their feet on the cabin's roof, each grabbed hold of the round handle.

"Stephen, look!" Littman yelled.

The planes had turned around and were coming back.

"They must have seen us!" Bartlett as he looked toward the south.

"Or they are returning to their base!" Littman reasoned.

Both men flattened themselves against the roof of the cable car, grabbing hand-rails that had been attached by the manufacturer as additional safety precautions.

While they watched, the planes flew overhead without changing course.

"Praise God!" Bartlett shouted, sighing expansively as the planes disappeared into the distance.

"Not so quickly, Stephen . . . ," he heard Littman say.

Bartlett jerked his head around and faced the other man.

A pistol.

Littman was pointing a pistol at him.

"Your expression is all the wonderful applause that someone such as myself could ever need," he said. "I fooled you completely."

"You're a double agent, aren't you?" Bartlett guessed.

"Bravo, Stephen. And you know what? I am not even Jewish!"

"You seemed familiar to von Tresckow because he saw you in the same play with the Führer's impersonator. Am I right?"

"Impressive," Littman admitted. "You look rather dumb in the way so many other Americans do, like half-witted farmhands who have stepped into something that is simply beyond them. It surprises me that you have caught on so quickly."

"The reason he didn't remember you right off is that he was captivated by the other man, so he blocked out everything else, everything but the plan he thought of that night."

"I must take your word for that, Stephen."

"You never contacted any partisans, did you, when you left to use the shortwave equipment? You were in touch with Berlin instead."

"Applause is due *you* this time. Forgive me, though, if I do not offer it. I need this weapon *and* I have no wish to slide off this cabin."

"All that talk about Jewish pain, Jewish loss, Jewish hatred toward the Third Reich? It was fake, an act?"

"Written by Goebbels himself . . . perhaps my finest script, Stephen."

"If you kill me now, you're still stuck out here in the middle of—"

"Nice try. I have always been prepared to die for the Fatherland. It might as well be here as opposed to a customary battlefield."

Littman raised the pistol slightly, aimed it at Bartlett's forehead.

"Good-bye, Stephen Bartlett. May you join the *Juden* scum in hell!"

Bartlett's gaze darted for a split second to his left.

"One of the planes is returning, Anton," he warned. "The pilot probably doesn't know about you. Even if he did, there is no way you *could* be recognized from a distance."

"Not so clever," Littman growled. "You can't distract me so easily."

"I'm telling you the truth. But then someone who lies about Jewish blood in his veins can't be expected to know what truth is. You were *too* convincing, Anton. I think your mother or your father was Jewish and you don't have the guts to admit it. *You're a coward as well as a liar!*"

Littman let out a scream and raised himself slightly. As he stretched his gun arm in front of him, toward Bartlett, he shouted something at the American, but the sound of a fighter plane's engines drowned him out.

And a dozen bullets machine-gunned into his chest, tearing him open and throwing him backward, off the roof, and into the valley below.

The plane started to turn around and head back toward the cable car.

Bartlett dropped back through the opening and down into the cabin.

"Littman betrayed us!" he told the others.

"Stephen, the plane!" Clerkin said as he glanced through the large window facing in that direction.

"On the floor!" Bartlett ordered.

They all fell immediately.

Bullets strafed the top of the cabin, sending bits and pieces of the roof down over them.

"Holy Mother of God! Look!" one of the pilots uttered as he half-stood and glanced through the window on the opposite side. "It's not finished . . . it's coming *back* after us!"

"Wouldn't you do the same thing if you were firing at a Nazi target?" another said.

A second barrage made the cabin tilt to one side, everyone sliding toward that end as though they were in a ship sinking at sea.

"The gears connecting us to the cable must have been hit!" Clerkin surmised. "If he tries a third time, we're dead and buried!"

Seconds passed.

No evidence of engine sounds nearby.

And then, all too familiar, sounds from the fighter plane were heard again.

Abruptly an explosion shook the cabin from side-to-side, shattering one of the large windows and the frame surrounding it.

Andrew Bartlett was blown toward that gaping hole.

His father couldn't reach him in time. Ernie Clerkin grabbed the boy's arm just as he went over the edge and yanked him back into the cabin but to do that he had to half-stand. Another wrenching motion knocked him off-balance and he fell through the opening himself, a scream tearing past his lips.

Momentarily the cabin's motion ceased. And for a little while, no one could speak.

"Someone blew that fighter out of the air!" Bartlett called out. "But we still have a struggle ahead of us."

Some wind suddenly kicked up, again swaying the cabin less than gently, then stopped.

"We can stay here," he continued, "hoping that someone will come to get us but that is hardly likely. It's more likely that any connections left to the cable above won't last very much longer, and on top of that, we can't be sure about another pass by one of those other fighter planes, particularly now that a comrade has perished," Bartlett said.

"So we climb out and make our way along the cable to the other side?" one of the remaining pilots asked.

"We have a chance if we do that," Bartlett concurred.

As he looked at Natalie and Andrew beside him, he added, "But it's nothing more than a slight chance at best. We can't be sure the cable will permit this. It could prove to be too much stress for it."

He glanced from face to face.

"However, I feel that we must try," he stated emphatically. "Agreed?"

Everyone shouted affirmation.

Partisans and others in "disagreement" with the Nazi regime had been filtering over the Swiss border for years. But almost never had they launched an attack against Germany from Swiss soil. It happened occasionally, but when it did and the offenders were caught, they were either imprisoned for long terms because their conduct struck at the heart of Swiss neutrality, or they were sent to Germany, depending upon the circumstances.

The downing of the German fighter plane by an anti-tank bazooka was one of the more serious instances of Swiss-based resistance. The handful of partisans responsible reacted by dancing wildly and boisterously sharing a bottle of French champagne, warm though it was, champagne appropriated by the Nazis and now in the hands of this band of roving Jews and Czechs.

They were well into this outburst of celebration when one of their members returned from his lookout post to their little temporary settlement of pitched tents. Before he could speak, the rest, glad to see him, urged that he join in with them.

"We cannot!" he insisted. "Those people need our help!"

"You are daft," another replied. "No one could be left alive."

"You are wrong. Come! See!"

Several joined him as he returned to the lookout area that was his responsibility at that late hour in the day.

"Here!" he exclaimed, thrusting his binoculars toward them.

One by one, they did what he asked, and found out how correct he had been to plead for help—survivors were climbing from the shattered cable car to the cable itself, and then inching along it like human ants on a metal rope.

They needed to know nothing more.

25

They could hear individual wires, spun together to form the cable, starting to break with a *whooshing* sound as each slashed through the air. Every time another went, they knew, their weary little group was that much closer to the rest snapping under their weight.

Stephen Bartlett had taken the belt from Andrew's trousers and secured each end of it around his son's wrists. If the boy should lose his grip on the cable, he wouldn't fall immediately although continued pressure by tough leather against those thin wrists of his would quickly cut off the circulation of blood and—

No! he screamed to himself. *Not when we're so close to asylum!*

Bartlett shook his head, dismissing that thought from his mind. He took his own belt and used it on his wife's wrists in the same manner. Although she was a hearty woman, active and strong, not accustomed to a cloistered and pampered life, she could not hold on indefinitely, not like men trained in such survival techniques. Perhaps, in their exhausted and weakened condition, if Natalie and Andrew fell they would possess insufficient strength to pull themselves back up to the cable and drape their legs over it as they inched along its length. But at least he could try to reach them before the belts broke under their weight, try to help before they fell away and were smashed against the rocks below.

Another wire strand in the cable snapped. This one flew off into the valley below. Seconds later, yet another strand split loose but did not break away. Instead it flew back, burying itself like a striking scorpion into the hand of the pilot at the end of the line, a younger one whose name had gone unannounced. He screamed in pain and had to relinquish his hold, dangling by only his other arm.

In front of Bartlett was his family. He couldn't turn around. He could only watch, helpless, as the young man weakened and in an instant was gone, despite the efforts of the pilot ahead of him to reach back and grab his comrade before it was too late.

Only thirty feet more.

Only—

The cable snapped altogether.

As it did, two of the three remaining pilots slid down its abbreviated length, frantically trying to tighten their grip on what remained of it.

Gone.

Only one pilot was now left alive.

The cable slammed against the side of the mountain.

"Andrew!" his wife screamed as she saw her son hit a large outjutting boulder, cushioned by a large section of overhanging moss-like growth.

The motion of the cable spun the boy in her direction, and she noticed blood streaming from his broken nose.

"Use my shoulders, Andrew!" she told him, trying to ignore the pain that was lancing through her own body. "Rest your feet on them, *please!*"

"Mom, Mom, I can't hold on," he called to her. "I hurt too much. I—"

His mother's eyes widened as she glanced just above Andrew and tried to shout something to him, but he couldn't hear what she said. Finally, having to let go, whatever strength he had now dissipated, he cried as he started to fall, "Mom, Dad . . . don't ever forget that I love you so much!"

And then a large, weathered hand caught the eight-year-old in midair, and the boy looked suddenly up into the face of a man with a big smile crossing his scarred and bearded features before unconsciousness carried Andrew Bartlett's exhausted little body away in its comforting grasp.

Epilogue

After being given some food and water, Stephen Bartlett, his family, and the surviving pilot were led to the edge of a Swiss army outpost by the partisans, who bade them farewell and disappeared into the woods without ever giving their names. Less than a week later, after being treated at a renowned Swiss hospital, the Americans were driven to a clandestine meeting in a remote valley some miles outside Geneva at a spot that, decades later, would come to be known as L'Abri. They boarded an awaiting American aircraft to begin the uncertain journey back to England, arriving in the middle of the night after surviving an earlier gauntlet of intense German anti-aircraft fire.

Field Marshal Erwin Rommel eventually died by his own hand minutes before being taken into custody by the Gestapo after being falsely implicated in the July 1944 plot to assassinate Adolf Hitler at Rastenburg (in English, *Wolf's Lair*), a plot in which he had refused to take part.

Major General Henning von Tresckow likewise took his own life in order to keep from being tortured into revealing details of the complex underground Resistance movement he had helped to organize. By this sacrifice, he saved the lives of scores of co-conspirators in the German military as well as the Berlin political establishment and diplomatic corps.

Lina Heydrich chose to become an obscure figure, strictly adhering to the task of keeping her children away from any press attention, intent as she was on fashioning for them a normal life as free of the tainting residue of Nazism as possible. Despite these intentions, when anyone mentioned her husband's name, she would continue to speak of him as "my beloved, whom I miss each day of my life."

And then there was *Reischführer* Heinrich Himmler, who, during the closing months of World War II—but, of course, that is another story for another time . . .